CARTER
&
ARIA

WWINTERS
USA TODAY BESTSELLING AUTHOR

I should've known she would ruin me the moment I saw her.
Women like her are made to destroy men like me.
I couldn't resist her though.
Given to me to start a war; I was too eager to accept.

But I didn't know what she'd do to me. That she would
change everything.
She sees through me in a way no one else ever has.
Her innocence and vulnerability make me weak for her and
I hate it.
I know better than to give in to temptation.

A ruthless man doesn't let a soul close to him.
A cold-hearted man doesn't risk anything for anyone.
A powerful man with a beautiful woman at his mercy … he
doesn't fall for her.

MERCILESS

Preface

Carter

"I should have fucked you so much sooner."

I remember that first day, how she screamed and cried for me to let her go, back when I hated her and she hated me.

Even with my tight grip on her throat, with my touch sending sparks through her body , she forces her head to shake, not taking her eyes off of mine.

"No," she whispers and my dick hardens even more, begging me to punish her for daring to defy me. But then she adds, "This is how it was supposed to be."

Her breathing is heavy as she closes her eyes, her body bowed on my lap. She's completely at my mercy and her pouty lips are there for the taking.

All of her. Every piece of her is mine and she knows it.

Mine.

CHAPTER 1

CARTER

War is coming.

It's something I've known for over two years.

Tick-tock. Tick-tock.

A tic in my jaw clenches in time with the rhythm of the clock, while the skin over my knuckles turns white as my fist squeezes tighter. Tension rises in my stiff shoulders and I have to remind myself to breathe in deeply and let the strain of it all go away.

Tick-tock. It's the only sound echoing off the walls of my office and with each pass of the pendulum, the anger grows.

It's always like this before I go to a meet. This one, in particular, sends a thrill through my blood, the adrenaline pumping harder with each passing minute.

My gaze drifts from the grandfather clock in my office to the shelves next to it, then beneath them to the box made of mahogany and steel. It's only three feet deep and three feet tall by six feet long. It blends into the wall of my office, surrounded by old books.

I paid more than I should have simply to put on a display. All any of this is merely a façade. People's perceptions are their reality. And so I paint the picture they need to see so I can use them as I see fit. The expensive books and artworks, polished furniture carved from rare wood... All of it is bullshit.

Except for the box. The story that came with it will stay with me forever. In all the years, it's one of the few memories I can pinpoint as a defining moment. The box never leaves me.

The words from the man who gave it to me are still so fresh, as is the image of his pale green eyes, glossed over as he told me his story.

About how it kept him safe when he was a child. He told me how his mother had shoved him in it to protect him.

I swallow thickly, feeling my throat tighten and the cords in my neck strain at the recollection. He set the scene so well.

He told me how he clung to his mother, seeing how panicked she was. But he did as he was told. He stayed quiet in the safe box and could only listen while the men murdered his mother.

He offered to barter for his life with the box. And the story he gave me reminded me of my own mother telling me goodbye before she passed.

Yes, his story was touching, but I put a gun to his head and pulled the trigger regardless.

He tried to steal from me and then pay me with a box as if the money he embezzled was a debt or a loan. William was good at thieving, at telling stories, but the fucker was a dumb prick.

I didn't get to where I am by playing nicely and being weak. On that day, I took the box that saved him as a reminder of who I was. Who I needed to be.

I made sure that box has been within my sight for every meeting I've had in this office. It's a powerful reminder I can stare at as I make deal after deal with criminal after criminal and collect wealth and power in this godforsaken room.

It cost me a fortune to get this office exactly how I wanted it. But if it were to burn down, I could easily afford to replace everything.

Everything except for that box.

"You really think they're going through with it?" I hear my brother, Daniel, before I see him. The remembrance fades in an instant.

It takes a second for me to be conscious of my facial expression, to relax my jaw and let go of the anger before I can raise my gaze to his.

"With the war and the deal? You think he'll go through with it and take her tonight?" he clarifies.

A small huff leaves me, accompanied by a smirk as I answer, "He wants this more than anything else. He said they set her up and it's already happening. Only hours until they're done."

Daniel stalks into the room slowly, the heavy door to my office closing with a soft kick of his heel before he comes to stand across from me.

"And you're sure you want to be right in the middle of it?"

I lick my lower lip and stand, stretching as I do and turning my gaze to the window in my office. I can hear Daniel walking around the desk as I lean against it and cross my arms.

I tell him, "We won't be in the middle of it. It'll be the two of them, and our territory is close, but we can stay back."

"Bullshit. He wants you to fight with him. He's going to start this war tonight and you know it."

I nod slowly, the memory of the smell of Romano's cigars filling my lungs at the thought of him.

"There's still time to call it off," Daniel says, and it makes my brow pinch and forehead crease. He can't be that naïve.

It's the first time I've really looked at him since he's been back. He spent years away. And every fucking day I fought for what we have. He's gone soft. Or maybe it's Addison who's turned him into the man standing here now.

"This war has to happen." My words are final, and the tone is one not to be questioned. I may have grown this business on fear and anger, each step forward followed by the hollow sound of a body dropping behind me, but that's not how it started. You can't build an empire with bloodstained hands and not expect death to follow you.

His dark eyes narrow as he moves closer to the window, his gaze flickering between me and the meticulously maintained garden several stories below us.

"Are you sure you want to do this?" His voice is low, and I barely hear it. He doesn't look back at me and a chill flows across the back of my neck and down my arms as I take in his solemn expression.

It takes me back to years ago. Back to when we had a choice and chose wrong.

When whether or not we wanted to go through with any of this still meant something.

"There are men to the left of us," I tell him as I step forward and close the distance between us. "There are men to the right. There is no possible outcome where we don't pick a side."

He nods once and slides his thumb across the stubble on his chin before looking back at me. "And the girl?" he asks, his piercing eyes reminding me that both of us fought, both of us survived, and we each had a tragic path that led us to where we are today.

"Aria?" I dare to speak her name and the sound of my smooth voice seems to linger in the space between us. I don't wait for him to acknowledge me—or her, rather.

"She has no choice." My voice tightens as I say the words.

Clearing my throat, I brace my palms against the window, feeling the frigid fall beneath my hands and lean forward to see Addison beneath us. "What do you think they would have done to Addison if they'd succeeded in taking her?"

His jaw clenches, but he doesn't answer my question. Instead he replies, "We don't know who tried to take her from me."

I shrug as if it's semantics and not at all relevant. "Still. Women aren't meant to be touched, but they went for Addison first."

"That doesn't make it right," Daniel says with indignation in his tone.

"Isn't it better she come to us?" My head tilts as I pose the question and this time he takes a moment to respond.

"She's not one of us. Not like Addison, and you know what Romano expects you to do with her."

"Yes, the daughter of the enemy…" My heart beats hard in my chest, and the steady rhythm reminds me of the ticking of the clock. "I know exactly what he wants me to do with her."

Chapter 2

Aria

There are a few things you should know about me.

I like to wake up with a hot cup of coffee every morning. Preferably with enough creamer and sugar to drown out the taste of the bitter caffeine addiction.

I love red wine at night. I can't have white; it gives me a headache and a hangover that will leave me miserable when I wake up.

Well, those aren't things that really matter. They're the superficial details you give people when you don't want to tell them the truth.

What do you really need to know?

My name is Aria Talvery and I'm the daughter of the most violent crime family in Fallbrook.

The reason I like to have wine at night is because I desperately need it so I can get a few hours of sleep.

My mother was murdered in front of me when I was only eight years old and I've never been okay since then, although I've learned to be good at pretending I am.

My father's a crook, but he kept me safe and tolerated me even though every day he reminded me how much it hurt him to look at my face and see nothing but my mother.

It's because of my eyes. I know it is.

They're a hazel-green concoction, just like hers were. Like the soft mix of colors you'd see in a deep neck of the woods when looking up at the canopy of leaves in late summer, early fall. That's how my mother used to describe it. She was poetic that way. And maybe some of that rubbed off on me.

Fact number... whatever we're on: I love to draw. I hate the life I live and hide away in the sketches and smeared ink. Away from the madness and danger my existence inherently brings.

And that love of art, the one thing I have that still connects me to my mother, is why I ended up at this bar, tracking down the asshole who stole my sketchbook from me. The prick who thinks he's funny and that I'm some stupid joke or a toy he can play with because I'm a woman living in a man's world, a dangerous one at that.

But I inherited my temper from my father. And that's why I ended up at the Iron Heart Brewery on Church Street. Yes, a bar on a street called "church." What's more ironic is how much sin has seeped into these walls.

And so I went willingly, after my precious notebook that was stolen and walked right into the enemy's arms.

It was a setup, but my mother would have called it kismet. You should know I'm smiling now, but it's a sarcastic smile as a huff of feigned laughter leaves me. Maybe all of this is her fault to begin with. After all, that notebook was irreplaceable to me because the only picture I had of her was tucked into the spine.

The last thing you should know, and the most important of them all, is that I refuse to break. I don't give in and I don't back down. Not for anyone, and especially not for Carter Cross. The bastard who took me from my family. Locked me in a room and told me in simple words that my life was over, and I belonged to him.

It won't be his cutting words from his sharp tongue. Or his broad shoulders and muscular arms that pin me down and trap me. It won't be his charming smile that utters filthy words that makes me cave. And it won't be that spark in his eyes, the flames licking and flickering brighter and hotter every time he looks at me.

No, I refuse to give in. Even if that same heat echoes in my chest and travels lower.

But there's this thing about breaking; the more you harden yourself and try to fight it, the easier and sharper the snap is when you inevitably break.

And I know this all too well.

The day my life changed forever...

There's a constant ringing in my ears. My fists are clenched so tight that my knuckles have turned white. Every time I have to face these assholes my father works with, this is how it feels.

Like I'm on edge.

My heart thuds, thuds, thuds as I pass the all-glass front door to Iron Heart Brewery and keep walking like I'm not going in. The front exterior is all windows, so they can easily see who's coming and going; bulletproof, too. Because of the clientele. Word is my father fronted that bill, but that seems overly generous for a man like him.

Cold. Selfish. Greedy. That's how I'd describe my father, and I hate myself for it.

I should be grateful; I should love him. But I'm loyal at least, and loyalty is all that matters. When you grow up in this life, you learn that little tidbit quickly.

Resting my shoulder against the dark red brick just past the windows, I take a look at the parking lot across the street. They aren't here yet.

A frustrated breath leaves a trail of fog in the tense fall air as I cross my arms.

This is where my father's men go on a night off and I know Mika is going to be here.

I hate being here alone, but I can't wait for someone to save me. I hope Nikolai will come with them too. He's a childhood friend, although now a soldier of my father's, and my saving grace. Really, he's my only friend and he's put that bastard Mika in his place more than once when my father wasn't there for me.

Even knowing that to be true, that if Nikolai comes there won't be any problems in the least, I hate that I have to be here at all. My thumb runs along the tips of my cold fingers, remembering how I held the notebook only moments before Mika came into the room. The photograph was tucked safely inside. Waiting for me to be inspired by it.

A notebook is only a notebook, but that photograph is the only one I have of my mother and me the year she died.

My father didn't have time for my "meaningless shit," as he called it, and the vise around my heart tightened at his response.

A shiver runs down my shoulders and I let out another heavy breath. I can feel the chill on my nose and cheeks. My thin jacket isn't doing a damn thing to help me. I hadn't realized fall had come with intentions of revenge on the smoldering summer.

Peeking up through my lashes, I read the chalkboard sign

above the bar through the windows. They're all locals, all drafts. I guess I could have one drink while I wait.

The smooth music hits my ears as I walk into the bar, my heart beating faster as I take in a few of the men seated on the stools. It's funny how a bar being mostly empty sends greater fear through me than one that's packed. One where I can blend in.

Right here, right now? I don't belong, and every soul here knows it.

Maybe this is why Mika thought he could get away with it, I think bitterly as I try to ignore the scared little girl inside of me. He thinks he can steal from me because my father won't stop him and I'm too spineless to even come out of my room unless called upon.

I force myself to straighten my back as I move closer to the bar and set down my clutch. I have a plan and I go over it as I try to swallow, form a smile, and order a drink.

"Vodka and Sprite," I order easily as I slip onto the barstool and meet the bartender's eyes. With a nod he moves seamlessly to the glasses, making them clink and then filling one with ice.

I'll wait for the guys. Even if they scare me because I know what they're capable of. I'll look Mika in the eyes and tell him to give my sketchbook back to me by tomorrow. And then I'll walk away. No threats. It's a simple request. He wants to play around and tease me and I won't give him the time to do so.

That's the only reason he took it.

He gets a thrill from goading me.

The wind batters against the glass windows to my right and it startles me. None of the men lining the room seem to have noticed it.

I'm too busy watching the hanging sign for the brewery banging against the window that I don't see the bartender come up to me.

The sound of the glass hitting the hard maple bar top sends a spike of fear through me and I jump in surprise.

The sudden stillness and immediate silence that accompanies all of their eyes on me force me to tense. I can barely form a smile as I stare straight ahead and thank the bartender.

First, I feel a rush of embarrassment, followed by fear that they know I'm weak. Then that all-consuming anxiety that everything is going to go wrong washes over me. Very wrong.

It makes me want to throw up, but instead, I lift the cold glass to my lips. One sip of the sweet cocktail does nothing. Two, and my throat still feels dry.

I'm a foolish girl. I lick a bit of soda from my bottom lip and set the glass down on the counter as I stare at all the colorful labels of liquor bottles lining the shelves.

There's no one who will stand up for me and I can't even bring myself to think about confrontation without getting jumpy. Trying to swallow proves useless and so I push myself off the stool with both hands clinging to the cold bar.

My palms are clammy, and I nearly tell the bartender I'm just going to the restroom as if he'd care. As if anyone cares.

That feeling of complete insignificance follows me with each step to the left of the bar as I head down a skinny hallway. It's the only way to go, so the restrooms must be there. I only make it a few steps before I think I hear a shot. My body tenses and my heart goes still. It knows that if it were to beat, I wouldn't be able to hear a single thing else.

There's no scream. There's nothing but the sound of the music. I must have only thought I heard one. It's all in my head.

My eyes close as I will myself to breathe. But then they bolt open at a familiar noise.

It's not the harsh sound of a gun going off. It's the whiz of a gun with a silencer, followed by the thud of a body hitting the floor.

Bang, bang! Two of them back to back, and this time everything sounds closer. Another shot. My body clings to the wall as if it can hide me.

I force myself to move, to head to the back and find a way out or place to hide. I might be a scared little girl, barely surviving in my father's world, but I'm not a fucking idiot.

I quicken my pace as I round the corner, motivated by the sheer will to live. But every bit of strength I have, even if it is minuscule, is for nothing.

The scream that's torn from my throat is barely heard as

a thick bag covers my head.

My clutch falls to the floor, hitting my thigh as I kick out and miss the man in front of me. My heels go with it, each kick accompanied by the rough laughter of several men.

I try to fight, but it's no use.

It's more than one man, I know that. Their hands are strong and their bodies like bricks.

I don't stop and won't, but nothing I do is helping. I punch and yell and kick as terror flows through me, begging me to push them away and run. I can't see, and my arms scream in pain as they're pinned behind me.

I only know we're outside because of the wind slicing through my thin jacket. I only know I'm in a trunk because of the telltale sound of it opening before I'm tossed in, my small body crashing against the back of it as it's quickly shut.

Silence.

Darkness.

My breathing is ragged, and it makes me lightheaded.

When my screaming stops, my voice is hoarse, and my throat burns with harsh pain every time I try to swallow. When my banging ends, my wrists are rubbed raw and cut from the cuffs and my muscles are aching with the type of pain that's scorching hot and forces me to tremble.

Another feeling takes over. It's not quite panic. It's something else.

It's not a sense of hopelessness. Not that either.

When you're alone and you know nothing is okay and nothing's going to be okay, there's this feeling that's overwhelming and inescapable.

My heart keeps ticking along despite everything. But it's going too fast. Everything is going too fast and it hurts. And I can't stop it. I can't stop any of it.

When you've done everything you can, and you're left with nothing but fear of both the unknown and the known, there's only one way to describe it.

That feeling is true terror.

CHAPTER 3

CARTER

"**Y**ou're going to keep her here?" It's not much of a question from my brother; more of a statement as he looks around the cell. Jase was the middle child of five boys and never learned how to start a conversation without being direct and blunt. I suppose I can't blame him. The thought reminds me of Tyler. The fifth brother who died years ago. His memory numbs the reality of the present, but only for a moment.

Jase leans against the far wall with his arms loosely crossed and waits for me to answer.

We leave in only an hour. Each small tick of the Rolex on my wrist reminds me that I'm so close to having her. Only time separates us now.

Glancing from the thin mattress lying on the floor to the

metal toilet on the other side of the cell, I tell him, "I think I'll add a chair."

His quizzical expression only changes slightly. He may not even realize it, but I see it on his face. The disappointment. The disgust. I can hear the unspoken question that lingers on the tip of his tongue as he shifts his gaze from me to the steel door behind us. *When did you become this fucked up?* He has no idea.

"I'll need a place to sit." I keep my voice even, almost playful as if this is a joke. It's Jase though, and he knows me better than anyone. Much better than either Daniel or Declan. The three of them and I make the four Cross brothers. But out of all of us, Jase and I are the closest.

As much as I can hide the anxiousness of getting my hands on Aria from everyone else, he can see it. I can tell by how careful he's been around me since I told him.

"How long?" he asks me.

"How long what?"

"Will you keep her here?"

"As long as it takes." *For what?* The question is there in his eyes, but he doesn't ask it and I have no intention of telling him regardless. I could lie and tell him as long as it takes for the war to end. As long as it takes to see if she'll be useful in negotiations if Talvery wins. The lies could pour from me, but the truth is simple. As long as it takes for me to decide what I want from her.

"There's no shower," he remarks.

"There's a faucet by the side of the toilet and a drain. She'll figure it out while she's in here."

Time passes and a chill settles in the already cold air. I know this is something I've never done, and it crosses more than one line. But in times of war, there is no right and wrong.

"I could give her other things. Little by little." Although I'm answering his question, I'm merely thinking out loud.

"Last time I was here, I was getting some very useful intel," Jase comments as he moves to the corner of the room. I know he's looking at the rim of the drain, inspecting it for any remnants of the blood.

The cell has only been used for one thing prior to this. It's what Jase excels at.

"Are you planning on getting information from her?" Jase asks with genuine curiosity and before I can answer he quickly adds, "I don't think Talvery is known for speaking business openly."

I would commend Jase for prying, but this isn't a matter I want him or anyone else involved in. She's mine and mine alone in this deal. And I'll do whatever I want with her. My brothers and everyone else can go fuck themselves where she's concerned.

"No, I don't think she knows anything."

Jase walks casually around the small room. Ten feet by ten feet. That's more than enough space. His boot brushes against the mattress and then he kicks it. There are no springs or coils in the thing. There's nothing in here she could use as a weapon.

I made sure of that.

"Just a mattress and a chair?" he asks, still skirting around the questions he wants answered. After years of me leading us and making the decisions, he knows better than to question me, but this is fucking killing him. It's eating him alive that he doesn't know what I want to do with her or why I want her. And the knowledge that it's killing him only thrills me.

"For now. I imagine she's going to want to fight and the fewer things in here, the better."

"And you think this is a sign that we can trust the Romanos? He gives you the girl, risking everything to get her, and you trust him to go to war? If he really has her and is willing to hand her over to you?" He's reaching, prying still.

"We can't trust anyone." I make sure he holds my gaze as I add, "That truth will never change." We only have each other. That's how we survived, and that's the only way we'll continue to live.

He's smarter than that. I imagine Jase will realize why all of this is happening before anyone else. That's his job, to gather any and all information necessary. By any means.

"Then this is a test?" he questions. His forehead is creased, a deep line evident. He's lucky he's my brother and that I still feel guilty for bringing him into this. For bringing all of them deeper and deeper into my hell I've created.

"The Romanos want the Talverys dead and vice versa. All over a decade-old feud for territory. The Romanos need allies and the upper hand. It was only a matter of time before I agreed to war; she just happened to be the first casualty. I wanted something, and Romano is going to give it to me, so we back him and not the Talverys."

"Casualty?" he asks to clarify if I really am going to kill her.

"You and I both know if she stays with her father, she'll die at his side... or worse," I say easily as I leave the cell. Jase's footsteps echo behind me.

"Why save her?" Jase's question echoes in my veins. Agreeing to take her is a risk I shouldn't have taken.

"It was an impulsive decision."

"It's unlike you," Jase pushes, and I have to steady my breathing to keep from telling him to fuck off. He has no idea that Aria once saved me. No one does, not even her. Whether I hate her for it, or something else, I have yet to decide.

"After this is over, what do we do with her?" Jase asks me.

Closing the steel door, I shut it tightly and pull the edge of the painting back over the barely visible slit of the frame. The door is designed to be concealed. If you didn't know how to maneuver the painting just so to unlock the hidden seal, you'd never see a door at all.

It's a soundproof cell no one would ever find. Impenetrable and fitted with an electronic cloak so any type of tracking is silenced. It's Aria's new home.

His question resonates with me as I turn my back to the cell. *What am I going to do with her afterward?*

"I haven't thought that far ahead," I reply, and the tone of my answer puts an end to his questioning.

CHAPTER 4

ARIA

My heart will kill me before these men do. That's all I can think as it races in my chest. I've never felt fear like this.

Maybe it's a lie that I've never felt it before. But it's been so long, and I don't remember my heart pounding like it is now.

My hot breath makes me feel faint as I try to breathe steadily. My eyes open even though all I can see is darkness with the bag still wrapped around my head.

I have to be smart. As much as I'd love to fight, I have to be smart or I'll die.

It's impossible to be smart when you're terrified though.

The dry lump in my throat feels scratchy as I swallow, opening my eyes to see nothing but the scant light that seeps through the burlap. I can't make out anything but I can hear everything. My erratic heartbeat blasting in my ears, the sound of several men in the room, and the scraping of chairs across the floor. One of them is named Romano and I'm fully aware that he's a man who hates my father. *I'm in the hands of the enemy.* I know I'm on a plastic tarp. I can feel the slickness beneath my fingers. It almost feels like a trash bag beneath me.

That's what scares me the most. I've never seen my father kill anyone, but I know they line the floor before they go through with it. It makes it easier for cleaning up.

I try to swallow again, gently lifting my head because I feel like I'm going to suffocate if I don't breathe.

"Bitch is up." My breathing hitches at the gruff voice coming from somewhere in front of me.

I tried and failed, not to let them on to the fact that I'm awake. Even when the cigar smoke woke me, and I thought I was in a fire, I was still. A few minutes have passed at most; I haven't learned shit that's going to help me though, other than that I'm lying on a floor and helpless.

Someone else responds, "Just in time." And then rough laughter erupts in the room.

My aching body stiffens, my hands clenching and making the cuffs dig deeper into my broken skin. I'm so terrified, I don't react to the pain shooting up my arms.

Every second that passes is agonizing. They speak calmly, softly, and in Italian. A language of which I know very few words.

I know *baldracca* though. It's the word for whore

and hearing that makes my shoulders hunch in a useless and pathetic effort to hide myself as a new sense of fear overwhelms me.

There's no doubt in my mind that I'm being held captive by one of my father's enemies. Romano, and he's one of many. I would give them anything to be able to run back home and stay there forever.

"Please," I can't help the attempt to bargain that slips from me. "My father will pay you whatever you want." The tears come without notice and my voice cracks on every other word. The warmth of my breath makes my heated face feel even hotter.

I've never thought of myself as such a weak person. But tied up and knowing my fate includes death or being a whore, the desperation outweighs anything else.

"There is no saving you Talvery trash," a man sneers as he walks closer to me with deliberate steps. His heavy footfalls get louder and quicker. Instinctively I try to back away, despite being on my side with my ankles and wrists cuffed behind my back. The struggle is useless. With my back against a wall and nowhere to go, all I can do is hunch my body inward as the heavy boot kicks brutally into my gut.

The air leaves me in a harrowing instant. Pain bursts inside of me, radiating outward but coiling in my stomach. It sinks deep inside of me, making me want to throw up to get rid of the agonizing pain.

I sputter and heave, trying my best to remain quiet. Bastard tears leak from my eyes and I can't stop them. I can't do anything.

This is a hell I've been terrified of for so damn long. A nightmare that I knew could be a reality. Helpless takes on a new meaning.

My body trembles and the fear is overwhelming. But then I remind myself, be quiet. Be smart. There is always hope. Always. I'm smart enough to find a way. The idea is soothing for a moment until I hear the boot rise again and my instinct to cower is greeted with laughter in the room.

I pray that maybe I'll wake up. Although I know it's not a possibility I'm asleep, because pain doesn't follow you to your dreams. Not this kind.

But the thought gives me a heady comfort that allows me to stay quiet as the men talk and laugh, their banter mocking me and my helplessness.

My father will come for me. That last thought I nearly whisper to myself. My lips mouth the words and I stay in the fetal position with my eyes closed.

He will save me.

It's his pride at risk. If for no other reason, stealing me is a sign of weakness for him. He won't allow it. My breathing slows at the thought, the adrenaline in my blood seemingly ebbing away from me. He has to save me.

"Do you think we should torture her first? Get any

information out of her?" The two questions are asked by another man farther away from me and on my left. One with a casual and lighthearted way about the fucked up questions which leads to the room being filled with Italian comments and some amused chuckle from my right.

Sweat covers my skin. Turning hot and cold as the air smothers me.

The laughter is silenced with the sound of the door opening and greetings are exchanged. Only three men speak, and I can't make out the words until the door is shut again.

Something's changed. The air in the room is different. I can feel it.

"Is that her?" a deep, rough voice asks. The velvet cadence of the man who interrupted the jovial laughter makes everything still. Goosebumps flow over every inch of my skin.

There's no answer for a moment, but I imagine someone may have nodded.

Again, my heart beats and I wish it would stop. I need to hear. All I can think is that I'm going to be slaughtered.

I can't be. Not like this. Please, God, not like this.

My adrenaline spikes and I can't help that my head turns to hear better. Everything in the room is still and so quiet that I can hear the puff of a cigar. It's so clear I can imagine his lips as he exhales, the deep breath overshadowing everything else.

"I didn't think you'd do it," the new man's voice says calmly and in control. The others had an accent to them, but this one is from here. American descent, born and raised. Still, his voice commands fear. There's something about it, the intonation that feels like power in and of itself. He says, "It's very rare that I'm proven wrong."

Fear and hope flow through me. The fear I expected, but hope doesn't make sense. It's alive in me though. Some part of me urges to beg the smooth-voiced man to save me as if it knows he's my savior.

"Aria Talvery." He says my name with reverence, but even so, as he steps closer to me, the tread of his shoes on the floor not nearly as heavy and foreboding as the man who kicked me, I instinctively move away.

I don't even notice how calm my heart is until he says the words that create utter chaos.

"The deal wasn't meant to be taken literally." A slew of Italian fills the room. Not everyone's yelling, I know that, but several are and their anger ricochets through the room.

"You said you'd do it; you'd side with me in the war in exchange for her. Are you going back on your word?" One voice is louder than the rest. Deeper and raspier. It sends a sickening chill through my bones.

"I didn't, actually. And terms need to be negotiated."

The man with the raspy voice responds quickly and doesn't hide his irritation as he retorts, "You've known about this for three days. Three fucking days!" He yells the last three words and they make me jump as much as I can in this position.

Speaking with nothing but control, the man who sent for me answers him, "Like I said, I didn't think you'd do it."

"*Bastardo,*" a new voice spits and it's followed by the crunching sound of a punch.

"Fuck!" another man yell, but I don't recognize his voice, and the sound of guns being cocked fills the room.

"Jase, no need."

My eyes are wide open as I lie helpless on the ground. My fingertips search for something, anything to help me but the only progress I'm making is pulling at the plastic beneath me.

Without any warning, three heavy steps come closer and the burlap bag is ripped off my head, taking a bit of my hair with it and forcing a scream from me. The bright light blinds me as I'm pulled up by the nape of my neck, clear off the ground and then hurled down to the floor.

I have no hands free to catch myself, they're still cuffed behind me and so my shoulder hits the ground first, then my face. The hint of blood fills my mouth, and pain shoots up my shoulder.

Fuck, it hurts. Everything hurts.

I rock onto my back as I cry out.

Please, make it stop. Please. I wish I could take myself away from here. I wish it were only a dream. But as my arm twists and scrapes on the cement in an effort to right myself, I know this is real. I can't escape this. I whimper and give into the pain. There is no nightmare to wake from. This is my reality.

"You said you'd back me if I gave her to you!" A violent scream tears through the small room. My neck cranes to see the man who spoke over a table. A rough and splintered, unfinished wood table. The man's dress shirt looks damp with sweat and his face glistens with it too. Dark, black eyes stare across the room toward me, but not looking at me. The anger on his face is undeniable and I can't look anywhere else as he screams words that make my body shudder with fear. "I won't let you go back on this!" My eyes close tight.

I've heard the whispers of war for years from man after man. It's been so long since I've actually feared the hint of it. Maybe that's where I made my first mistake. I forgot that I should be terrified and that the dangers are always lurking and waiting to strike.

Please take me far away from here. I can imagine this going wrong so quickly. I could be shot and never even given the chance to escape. My heart races wildly and the terror makes my body tremble.

"And now you've damaged her," the man, the one with control, says quietly and calmly but with an uncontained anger that's brimming with threats. The deadliness of his simple sentence silences the room once again. It's only then that I dare to open my eyes, slowly peeking up through my lashes.

Dark eyes stare deep into mine as a tall man crouches down in front of me. Not black like the other man's, not so darkened. But a mixture of browns and amber, like a piece of burned wood from a raging fire.

There's no heat there though. His eyes are so cold they make my blood freeze and instantly the air turns to ice. There's a hint of something in his gaze that speaks of inexplicable things. My body tenses, my lungs fear to move and I stay still like prey caught in the beautiful hunter's gaze.

Time passes slowly as he considers me. And I find myself hoping and praying that he'll save me. How ridiculous that I would, but there's something about his eyes. I can't refuse the pull, the electricity surrounding him that seems to bend the air between us, making me feel closer to him. So close that he could save me.

His intentions aren't any better than these men. But there's only one of him and he's a man of control. I prefer that to the chaos I'm currently in.

I know it. He can save me.

Even if it's only by killing me right now in this moment and ending the pain. And I'm acutely aware he could do it. There's not a thing about him that could hide the fact that he's a ruthless, cold-hearted killer.

His fingers brush along his stubble as he tilts his head, considering me. The sole light overhead, a bright light in the middle of the room casts a shadow down his face that somehow makes his chiseled and hard jaw look even sharper.

His presence alone speaks of a power that steals the air from me. I'm nothing beneath him as he towers over me. My eyes close slowly as he reaches out and gently brushes the hair from my face. His hot touch melts everything inside of me. It's tender but deliberate. The soothing caress makes me weaker as his fingers travel down my chin and to my throat.

His masculinity is undeniable, the fear of his power only adding to the forbidden desire that rages through me. The man is everything I've been taught to fear, although the sensation is mixed with something else entirely. Something I'd never admit.

And that's when he grips me, his fingers wrapping around my throat and forcing me to open my eyes, staring back into the dark abyss of his gaze.

CHAPTER 5

CARTER

"I asked for her, yes," I finally answer Romano although I'm still staring at Aria's face, those lips of hers parted and swollen from the fall as I tighten my grip just slightly. Anger ripples through me at the sight of the fresh wounds. That fucker put his hands on her. They hurt her. They hurt what's mine. The tic in my jaw spasms again as the rage intensifies. They should know better than to touch what's mine.

I force the boiling rage down to a simmer; I'm not a fool. There are six men in this room and only one is on my side. I'm not just outnumbered. I'm not prepared to fight. And I don't intend to either.

I want to take my gift and leave this prick to his war. I want that feeling back, humming in my veins. The sheer power of having her at my mercy, feeling her breath cut short and her blood rushing beneath my grasp. She's mine. Finally.

"But not for a beaten and broken version of her," I grit the words through my teeth and they come out lower than I expected. I'm barely contained as I loosen my grip, allowing her to break eye contact and suck in a deep breath.

If I hear another plea or whimper from her in reaction to this fucker, I know I'll shoot Romano without a second thought. And that can't happen. Not yet. The second I get my hands on Aria, her father will be after me. I need Romano to distract him just as much as Romano needs me.

Romano doesn't answer, and I imagine it's because my back is to him as I look over Aria. But he'll have to fucking deal with that. So long as she's here, she'll be looking at me and no one else.

I scan every inch of her and each time I see an injury, my teeth clench, and my muscles coil. The cut on her swollen lip. The scratches and scrapes around her wrists. There's a bruise on her arm and I'm sure there are more I can't see.

"We just got her two hours ago. She's not broken. You better not fuck me over." Romano's words are rushed and desperate as I stand tall, leaving the girl where she is.

My heart races, but I don't let on. To them, she's only a girl I randomly chose. A girl who was harder to kidnap. Just a challenge for them and nothing more.

"This isn't a fight or debate," I tell Romano with my back

still to him. I want him to know in his truest of hearts that I'm the one helping him, and it's only out of my desire to do so. He's fucked over more than one of his allies in the past. I'm going to make him think twice before he decides I can be used as a pawn.

Even knowing how much is at stake in this very moment, I can hardly think.

I can't pry my eyes from Aria. Her chest rises and falls steadily as she rolls onto her side. Her lips are a gorgeous hue of red. Her hair tousled and flowing over her bare shoulder. But what's better is how she keeps looking at me with a mixture of both fear and hope swirling in those striking hazel eyes. I didn't imagine she'd look like this. The sight is addictive.

"Plea-" she starts to say – to me - but Romano cuts her off. His sickening and desperate voice hushes the soft sounds of her speaking to me. My fists clench, nearly splitting the tight skin across my tense knuckles and instantly my suit feels like it's suffocating me. His ignorance will be the death of him.

"We had a deal and it will benefit both of us, Cross."

As I loosen my collar, walking closer to him in the filthy room, he continues, "You don't have to do anything but give me that territory, Carter." He raises his hands in defense when I stare daggers at him. "Only for a little while, just so we can strike first. You're closer to Talvery. You don't want your men to do the work, so what other choice do I have than to take it over?"

My gaze sweeps over a pile of crates in the corner of the room. There are three of them on top of empty pallets. The wooden table is etched and weathered. I can only imagine the blood and sweat and drugs that have seeped into the wood. Even over the smell of smoke, the stench is revolting.

Each man in the room is dressed similarly, except myself and Jase. I always wear a suit; it's better to overdress than under. Romano's attempt at an ill-fitting suit didn't last long. His wrinkled jacket is a puddle of cheap fabric laying across the back of his chair. The others wear nondescript hoodies and shirts with faded baggy jeans. Each of the thugs looks at me as I survey them, and each one of their questioning gazes falls without a word uttered from their insignificant lips.

And then I look back to her. Back to the soft curves of her waist, the messy halo of dark hair around her pale skin. Her slender throat that's so exposed as she writhes quietly and hopelessly on the ground. This beautiful, broken creature. She's all mine.

"Your men are positioned between Fourth and Weston, give that territory to me so I can take his men down." Romano starts to speak terms. "We'll take them all down at the same time on every edge of his territory. Any man who stands against us after that will die. It's simple. They back us, or they die like the rest of them."

"I've heard this all before," I mutter. He says he'll kill them all. Erase any trace of Talvery from our existence. It's related to unfinished business started a decade before me. All in the name of greed.

"Just give me access to that territory and the suppliers for the guns." He reeks of desperation as he adds, "That's what you agreed to!"

I expected a lot of things when I came here. But this amount of irritation is something I never accounted for. As the seconds pass, I imagine how I could kill each and every one of the men in this room. How long it would take. How many shots they'd get off. Jase is behind me and I know he could hold his own.

I have to will away the temptation and eagerness to get Aria alone. Leaving the image of her beautiful figure crumpled at my feet, I focus on the business at hand.

"You want me to back down, clear the path for your men?" I ask him.

"They'll never see it coming if we take them from both your side and mine. We take over on the edge of your territory--" I cut the fucker off before he can finish.

"He'll think it's me killing them off. When his men around the edge of my territory start dying, he'll come after me without a second thought." My words come out deadly. "This isn't me starting a war, it's you."

"I'm giving her to you for a reason." He rushes his words with sincere bewilderment.

"No deal," I say and turn to leave, but Aria's whimper

pierces through the air. Even without a word spoken, I can hear her plea not to leave her at their mercy. It does things to me that it shouldn't. Just the knowledge that the threat of my absence can create a reaction from her is everything to me in this moment.

"Wait!" Romano's hands smack on the wooden table in the center of the room. "What if," he swallows visibly as he pushes off the table and then lets out a heavy breath. I peek at Jase for the first time since we've been in here. In a slim-fitting suit and his arms hanging loosely in front of him, he could be the usher at a fucking wedding right now. Well, if it weren't for the glare on his face that can only be read one way, for anyone looking at him to fuck off.

"What if..." he pauses and clears his throat before looking me in the eye. "Once I take over Talvery's territory, we could split it." He earns himself a small reaction from me, the tilt of my head for him to continue. "I want to start flooding the product at the top, closest to just outside of the tri-state area, to keep the cops away from our bases."

"And?" I question him. "None of this is relevant to splitting a damn thing."

"I only need his territory in the Upper West Side. I don't even have enough men to cover the rest," he says in a lighter, nearly comical tone as if the problem's already been solved.

"I'm not interested in more territory," I state, and my barely spoken words cause the hopeful expression on his face to fade. "But I'd happily take a percentage of the profits to cover my losses," I offer. "Fifteen percent every quarter until my losses are paid."

"Deal." Romano is so quick to oblige, even his own men stare at him rather than at me. They can't be that stupid. An even-numbered war is never a good thing. They need men and territory and backing. I'll give them the minimum, and pray they still kill each other off.

I nod my head once. "Deal," I say and while forcing a semblance of a smile to my lips, I offer him an outstretched hand.

I have to keep the grin from spreading as I turn my attention back to the wide-eyed girl, still tied up on the floor. "Jase." I speak to my brother although I keep my gaze on her, "Put her in the trunk."

Chapter 6

Aria

It's odd, the things that you think when you're alone for hours in a room filled with nothing but hopelessness and anger. Some thoughts make sense of course.

Thoughts of Mika and how he should have been there. He should have been at the bar, and I find myself wondering if he knew. If he took my notebook because he knew how much I loved my art and I'd know he had it and come after him. I find it hard to believe he wouldn't expect me to go after it. Or else why do it? I've spent hours trying to determine the intentions of a psychotic asshole.

But the truth is that I wouldn't have gone after him for any other reason. I wouldn't have left the safety of home... if that picture hadn't been tucked safely inside.

The thoughts of Mika and how bleak my reality is seem reasonable.

Other thoughts though… other thoughts don't make sense.

Like the flashbacks of my mother.

I've been haunted by so many images of what happened the day she died for years now. But none of those keep me company as I rock on the cement floor in the corner of the cell.

It's the sweeter things I remember that are driving me mad.

My thumb brushes against the cut on my lip, sending a sharp pain through me that reminds me this isn't a dream.

"Aria," I hear my mother call out for me in the memory. I was hiding in the closet, so proud that I'd hidden so well. "Ria?" Her voice changed to fear and desperation, and my smile vanished. "Ria, please!" she begged as her hushed cry from the hallway beckoned me to show myself. My fingers gripped the door of the closet just as she forced the guest room door open. I remember how her light blue dress swung around her knees. How her perfectly pinned hair didn't come undone. Yet her voice and her bearing were nothing but distraught.

I wish I could go back to that moment. Where she was running toward me and so close. Where she'd inevitably be in reach.

"Don't hide from me." Her words were ragged as she pulled me into her chest. She rocked me too fast, she held me too hard before gripping my arms and making me look her in the eyes. I'll never forget how hers watered over. "You can't hide like that." Her words were so pained, they came out as only a whisper.

"I'm sorry, Momma," I tried to speak the words, so she knew I meant them. "I was only playing."

Tears leaked from the corners of her eyes as she pulled me back into her arms and rocked me.

She whispered many things, but the one that's stayed with me is that we don't live in a world where we can play.

I should have known better than to run after Mika.

Every possible situation of a setup runs through my head as I bite my thumbnail and rock against the cement wall. I can't sit. My legs beg me to run, but with nowhere to go, I simply stand and lean on the far wall across from the door. Waiting for it to open.

I was only playing myself, thinking that I could prove myself to be anything when I went to hunt down Mika. I was childish and foolish. I can hear my mother saying it now. How foolish she was, she said it all the time before she died. And foolish is what I've become.

I keep whispering that I'm sorry, and I know the man is watching me. Carter. That's what the men called him.

Carter Cross. I know he can hear my whispers of despair.

I'm not saying it to him though; it's an apology to my mother. I should have known better than to chase after the memory of her in that picture. The words are spoken as I focus on the metal drain in the corner of the room.

Between the toilet, mattress, and drain, I know this room is meant for prisoners, but also for torture and murder. One and then the other.

I've searched every inch; the sides of my hands are bruised from pounding against the tall steel door. There's simply no escape. One way in, and one way out.

I should have fought harder when Jase Cross, Carter's brother from what I overheard, held the rag to my mouth.

Stolen, drugged, and reassigned to a prison: that's what my life has become.

The faint sounds of the camera moving drag my attention back to it. It's the one thing in the room I wish I could destroy. There's only one from what I can tell, and it's in the far right corner of the room.

But the camera is encased in cement and untouchable, if throwing the metal chair was any indication. As I stare at the mattress, I wrap my arms around myself. I won't sleep on it; there's no way my back will ever touch it.

I suck in a deep breath, reliving the feeling of those dark eyes pinning me in place.

I know what he wants from me, but he'll have to fight me to get it. I'll kick him, bite him, scratch him until my nails break and bleed.

I'll make him regret this if it's the last thing I do.

My fingers lift slowly up to my jaw and then trail down

my throat. Remembering how his gentle comfort so easily became a threat.

My heart thumps hard, once then twice as I hear the fucking camera move again.

"What are you moving it for?" I scream out like a madwoman, as loud as I can. My throat is hoarse from the screaming before, my body screaming along with me in a shuddered breath.

"I'm not fucking going anywhere!" I scream again and then wrap my arms tighter around myself as I fall to the floor on my ass and then my side. Just the way I was when that monster first found me.

The cuts on the sides of my wrists touch the dirty cement floor. I should lie on the mattress. I know I should, even as my tearstained cheeks rest on the unforgiving floor.

If, for no other reason than to have the energy to fight another day. He's waiting me out, I think. And that's something I can't fight. Hours and hours have passed.

I don't know how much time has elapsed exactly, but I know I have to sleep. I can't stay awake forever, waiting for whatever's next.

I'm powerless and completely at Carter's mercy. And he's not even here. He had me stolen from my home, then nearly left me in the kidnapper's arms. And now that he has me, he's left me to go crazy on my own.

That's exactly how I feel as my heavy eyes stare at the steel door and sleep threatens to take over. When you don't know what's waiting for you, what you'll have to fight, it can do that to you. It can make you feel crazy.

Another hour passes, or more. So much time escapes and all my fight has gone. In its place, only fear and exhaustion remain.

"Why are you doing this to me?" I whisper as I stare at the camera, imagining all the answers it could give me. And not a single one of them offers me comfort.

I find it hard to believe that when I first heard his voice, I was so desperate for him to take me away. The blame lays on my survival instincts. The fear of what those men would have done to me made me desperate for Carter to steal me away. My mind drifts back to that moment, and I wish I'd looked harder for a different escape.

He's going to come back. And I need to be able to fight him. But how can I, when I don't know when he's coming, and I have to sleep? Eventually, I have to sleep.

I doze off once, at least once that I know of, and startle awake only to find myself aching on the floor. Forcing myself up, I try to open the door once again and then cry on the floor beneath it. I imagine him opening it in that moment, and that alone scares me to move to the farthest corner in the room.

How heartbreaking it is, that the only bit of comfort I have is knowing that when the monster comes back, I'll be as far away from him as I can possibly be. Even if it is only ten feet.

But it's what I needed to finally give in to sleep.

Of all the things to dream about, I dream of my mother.

And once again, I should have known better than to let my mind wander to the memory of her death.

CHAPTER 7

CARTER

S he fell asleep after fourteen hours of looking for an escape, slamming the chair into the door, screaming profanities, rocking against the wall, and whispering all her regrets.

And I watched every minute of it well into the early morning. Obsessed with what she'd do and watching the fight leave her as every hour passed.

After she'd realized her efforts were hopeless, she hummed softly. So low, that I thought it was only a buzz from the camera until I turned up the volume. She hummed for hours. I don't even know if she noticed.

She'd finally fallen asleep, the hum of a lullaby still soft on her lips. The thrill of victory sang in my blood.

It was only then that I left my office and the monitors,

reminding myself to be patient. I wouldn't be surprised if the carpet beneath my desk is worn from the pacing of my shoes against it.

My last thought as I left the office and checked the monitor on my phone, was that as much as she was fighting now, she'd cave. She'd give in and obey. She has no choice. And time is on my side. Not hers.

An hour into going through orders and updates on each of the deliveries, I heard her screaming again. But instead of it bringing the buzz of a challenge, her screams curdled my blood.

The sweat is still hot on my skin by the time I finally get to the cell and kick the door open with the gun cocked in my hand. My heart pounds in my chest. Aria's screams are violent and shrill.

I don't know what the fuck happened, who the hell got to her or how they got in here. But someone has their hands on her.

My heart hammers and the anger of her defiance is dulled by something primal, a raw fear that sends a prickle of unease through my body in an instant. I can hear the terror in her voice as she cries out into the dark room for someone to help her.

Someone's in there. Someone's hurting her. It's undeniable in her screams. I can't fucking breathe. I finally have her in my grasp. *Mine.*

My breathing is barely controlled with the gun raised in

the air above her place on the floor. Whoever it is will die a painful death for taking what's mine. "Please!" she cries out, her eyes shut tight as her body stiffens and her back arches on the mattress. She screams again, trembling, and helpless. Her small body is cradled into itself.

"Carter!" I hear Jase call out to me, the door to the cell still open. I can hear him running down the hall.

Now that the cell is open, anyone and everyone in here can hear her screams.

My gun lowers slowly as Jase enters the room behind me. His breathing is ragged as he closes the distance and stands next to me. Our shadows tower over her small frame, lying destitute in the bed. She doesn't stop crying out, and although she doesn't sob, the sounds are there.

She's captive to her dreams.

"Night terror," Jase says with a heavy breath. The metal of his gun rubs against his jeans as he slips it back into place and then looks at me. "I thought someone got in here." Tiredness is etched onto his face, but also the raw look of fear. He takes a moment to compose himself before starting to tell me, "I thought..."

As he starts to speak, she screams out again and the sharpness of the pain sends spikes over my skin that scrape their way down my body.

It's a desperate cry that sounds foreign to my ears, although I'm so used to hearing something similar. Pleas for mercy, which I never show.

"What do you want to do about it?" Jase asks me. He's still catching his breath, just like I am. I can feel him staring at me, wanting to know what to do next. I can't tear my eyes from her as she curls on her side.

Jase turns to the door as the sounds of someone else coming down the hall makes their presence known.

"I'll put her on the mattress," I tell him absently. "Take care of whoever that is and shut the door behind you," I order him, and my words come out flat. I try to keep the emotion away, but a sense of despair is evident. This wasn't a part of my plans. My fingers dip into my pocket, fingering the clicker that will open the door to the cell while I'm on the inside.

"You think they did something to her? Romano? Or maybe it's what she thinks is coming?" Jase asks and finally I turn to look at him.

"How the fuck would I know?" My words come out harsh. The anger at him suggesting her terror is caused by thoughts of what I'll do to her is unexpected and more than that, unwanted. Of all the things I expected from her, I didn't anticipate this.

It cuts me in a way I can't explain. I want to consume her every waking thought. I want her to live and breathe for me and my desires. And maybe this is the cost of it all. That I can have her during her days, but her nights will destroy her.

"Just a nightmare then," Jase says as if it's a casual

observation. The whimpers still slipping through her parted lips are accompanied with a strangled sound of pain.

"You aren't supposed to wake them, you know?" Jase breathes out. "When they have night terrors, you're not supposed to wake them up."

The light from the door is blocked and the shadow of someone else covers Aria's slender neck and bared shoulders. I don't turn to look, but I don't have to. It's Declan, asking what's wrong. He knew she was here, but he doesn't want any part of this.

"It's fine," Jase tells him and then continues, "I don't think you can do anything really."

"Just go," I tell them both and stand as still as I can as they leave the room, taking with them the light from the hall as the door shuts. The creak of the steel is met with a thud and then the click of the lock. It takes a moment for my eyes to adjust. Another moment of her small cries and then a scream. A terrified scream.

"What did I do that earned me this?" I question her although I know she can't hear. I haven't touched her; we haven't even started. I almost touch the cuts on her wrists, but I pull back. I'll give her ointment and bandages in the morning. She'll have to do it herself until she earns my touch.

"Please don't," she begs in her sleep. Her words are whispered so softly, and I wonder if they came out that way in her dream. "Please," she begs.

"You don't know what you're asking, songbird," I tell her softly and consider my own sanity in this moment. "You never had a choice. The moment your father left me alive, your fate was sealed," I confess to her. Something I've never said aloud to anyone.

He should have killed me. It's Nicholas Talvery's fault I'm allowed to live another day.

His fault... and someone else's. The moment the thought comes to me, I see her tremble. Beautifully weak on the cold, unforgiving ground, the sleep taking more and more of her as her words become quieter.

She worries her bottom lip between her teeth, and it's the only part of her that moves. *"Please."* Her lips mouth the word.

Kneeling before her, I'm slow and deliberate as I pick her up. Conscious of where my gun is tucked away in case she's playing me. She's light and fits easily into my arms. I thought she may fight me. That she'd react in fear to my touch. But instead, she molds her body to me and her slender fingers grip onto my shirt. Holding me tighter to her.

Her lips brush against the crook of my neck as I carry her the few feet to the mattress. Her pleas are still whispered, and the gentle warmth of her breath sends a tingle down my spine. I barely contain a groan of desire as I move her to the mattress. She clings to me still, holding tightly and begging me. This time she begs me not to leave her.

"Don't go. Stay with me... please," I barely hear her words.

Her face is still pained, but there's gentleness in her cries as I shift her onto the mattress.

Her hand fits in mine as I pull her fingers from me and place them on her chest. Her chest rises and falls as she calms herself, slowly drifting to a different place.

Time passes quickly. Too quickly as I sit on the mattress, making it dip with my weight and staring down at her. Her heavy sighs emphasize her breasts, the bit of lace from her black bra peeking from her shirt. It almost tempts me as much as the dip of her waist.

My gaze caresses each curve of her body as I remember the first time I heard her name.

The day my life changed forever.

Her bed groans in protest as Aria turns in her sleep, settling into the mattress and my body stiffens. I shouldn't be here right now. That's not how I gain the control I want. I can't breathe until she's still and her own breathing evens out. But as I move to stand, shifting my weight ever so slightly, the mattress slumps and her hand falls, her soft fingers brushing mine, the tips touching.

My hand stays still beneath hers, but it begs me to explore. To thread my fingers between hers. Closing my eyes and inhaling deeply, I remind myself that there is time.

Time will change everything.

My eyes open at the reminder. Just like that day did years ago.

The day my father dropped me off at the corner of West and Eighth by the liquor store to sell that last bit of his pain pills. I was more approachable, according to him and we needed to pay the bills. It didn't matter what I said or how much I didn't want to do it. I was the oldest of five, my mother was dead, and I had nothing left in me. Nothing but pain.

My father dropped me off on Talvery's territory unknowingly. And it wasn't long before I learned what it meant to sell drugs on his ground.

I was only a child before that day.

But one day changes everything.

CHAPTER 8

ARIA

Waking up with my heart beating out of my chest, the hope that it was all a nightmare crumbles into dust when all I can see is cement and cinder block walls.

I have to close my eyes and cover my face to keep from losing it. "This can't be happening." The trembling words leave my lips unbidden. Wrapping my arms around my knees, I try to tell myself that it's all a dream. I rock back and forth, and as I do, the sounds of the mattress creaking beneath me and the feel of my heels digging into the comforter makes my body freeze.

I try to remember last night, and I know full well I slept on the ground only a few feet away. I know I did.

My hands fly over my body. As if they could check to see

if I was touched.

I feel the sharp edges of a scratchy throat but swallow thickly, trying to suppress the terror of what he could have done to me.

I must have crept into the bed and not remember it. I know I haven't been touched. I would know, wouldn't I? "I would," I say the words aloud as if I was speaking to someone else. Maybe I just needed the reassurance. I don't remember a thing after falling asleep. I wish I could have just stayed awake.

The whispered words echo in the hollow room as I glance up at the door. And then to the camera as it moves. Carter Cross, I almost speak his name aloud. I've heard his name before, always spoken with anger. I know he's one of a number of brothers and the head of a drug cartel. That's where the information ends. My father never liked me knowing anything and the only bits I learned were slivers of the truth from Nikolai. And he only told me what I needed to know. They said it was to protect me, but I would give anything to know what I'm up against.

I'd give anything to know what Cross is capable of.

Is he just going to leave me here to die? My throat pains in a way I didn't think was possible.

"Let me out," my raspy voice begs and the words themselves are like knives raking up my throat. I haven't eaten or had a drink of water since I've been here, and I don't even know how long that's been.

I stand a little too quickly, and nearly fall as I try to make my way to the door. I'm dizzy, lightheaded, and I think I may throw up.

Still, I head straight for the door, pulling at the doorknob and desperately trying to open it. My fist slams against it, over and over.

There's no use, stupid girl.

Again, I slam my fist and scream out, "Let me go!" but I'm only met with an unmovable door in an empty room, with no way out and no idea of what will happen to me.

The pain from the next slam of my fist makes me wince and cradle my hand to my chest. My back presses against the door as I fall down slowly onto my ass, resting my head against the door.

So many slow moments pass. Moments where I just try to breathe. Moments where my fingers brush along the cuts at my wrists. Moments where I stand and stretch and pretend like it's not odd to stretch when you're caged like an animal. What's the point if there's no escape?

It takes me longer than it should to see the foam tray with a grilled cheese sandwich and the cup of water next to it.

And a bucket of water with a sponge behind it. I spent so much time staring at the door, I didn't see it.

He came in here.

He was here.

My chest heaves and again my fingers travel to my thighs. He didn't. I would know. I can barely contain the fear of knowing he came in here while I slept. It's hard to swallow and I stay far away from the tray of food.

Time slips by again. And then more time. There is no change in my predicament, save my sanity.

Although my stomach grumbles and the delicious scents of butter and cheese are all I can smell, I leave the tray where it sits.

I don't eat, and I don't undress to bathe myself. Not with him watching. The anger boils and rises to such an extreme that I almost slam the bucket across the room, straight at the camera.

I'm not his pet or his test subject. He can take that foam tray and go fuck himself with it. At least that's what I think when I first move closer to see it; the thought even gives me joy. Hours pass and then more. How much time, I don't know. There's nothing in this room and loneliness and boredom are only two of the emotions I'm not sure I'll be able to handle if this is how my new life will proceed.

My mind starts playing tricks on me and I find myself etching small things into the cinder blocks with a button on my shirt. The shirt's already ripped so it doesn't matter. The top two buttons have been pulled off, the first one long lost and the second now a writing tool. A small and poor one, but there's nothing else to do but pace and let my mind wander.

And that leads me to awful places.

I'm busy carving a pattern, a useless, meaningless pattern of birds and vines into a block that's not even deep enough to be seen clearly when the door opens behind me.

My heart lurches and I swing my body around so violently that the back of my head collides with the wall, the button slips from my hand and the sound of it pinging to a stop on the ground fills the room.

The flood of light is lost quickly as Cross steps inside my cell and closes the door behind him. His figure is like a shadow of darkness as he walks toward me.

"What do you want?" I ask instinctually, barely able to breathe, let alone swallow the pathetic words before I can speak them. I'm glad I didn't eat because if I had I would have lost it all in this moment. Panic rages inside of me.

He's quiet as he takes one step forward and then another. He only takes his eyes from me once, and that's to look at the chair in the corner of the room.

"My father will come for me," I tell him as he walks toward the chair and positions it so he can sit and face me. "He's going to kill you," I add, and my words are strangled, but audible.

All I'm rewarded with is a soft smile on his lips. The stubble on his jaw is more noticeable and his eyes seem darker, but maybe it's just the light. Everything else about him is more foreboding than I remember. His height and broad shoulders, the lean build of his body with the rippled accents of his muscles. God made him to do deadly, sinful things. One look and that's obvious.

As if reading my mind, he grins at me, forcing me to take a step back, which only widens the grin to a charming and perfect smile. I feel like I'm caught in a cage. A little mouse to a lion. And he's only toying with me.

"You're sick," I spit at him, clenching my hands into fists.

"I'm well aware of that little fact, Aria. Tell me, what else do you know about me?" His voice is smooth velvet, and it echoes in a deep way from wall to wall in the room. The kind of echo you feel deep in your gut, one that haunts you so much later in the night.

"I know my father will gut you," I answer him with sickening contempt.

"He isn't going to do anything. He doesn't even know I'm the one who has you." His head tilts slightly as he examines my every reaction.

"Yes, he does," I breathe as if it will be true if only I say it is. His look turns to pity, but only for a moment. It passes so quickly I wonder if I even saw it, or maybe it was only the dim light in the room playing tricks on me.

"He doesn't and even if he did, he's useless." Menace lingers on the heels of his words, falling hard and crashing to the ground around me.

He adds, "He couldn't even defend your mother's honor."

"Fuck you," I dare to sneer at him. Anger rises quickly inside of me and my breathing quickens.

"You fight now, but you'll submit later," Cross says easily, completely unaffected by my words.

"Submit?" the fear is evident in my voice.

"You'll do as I say. Every command. Kneel at my feet, undress, lie in my bed... Spread your legs for me." The depth of conviction in his voice is frightening.

"I'll die before I submit to you." My throat dries and tightens. I can barely breathe as he stands.

He's not quick, not hurried in the least to stalk toward me. I can run. I know I can, but the room is small; there's nothing to hide behind and he's so tall, it wouldn't take much beyond a lunge for him to catch me.

My knees weaken, and I nearly fall to the ground, but I don't. I stay as tall as I can although I have to crane my neck to look Cross in the eyes. My heart pounds chaotically as if it's trying to escape. For every step he takes forward, I take one back until I've hit the wall.

"How did you sleep?" he asks me in an eerily calm voice.

"Like a baby," I say, and my answer is nothing but defiant. I surprise myself with the immediate answer. Fuck him. Fuck Carter Cross.

A crooked smile twitches onto his lips. "Do you always have nightmares?" he asks and the strength inside of me wavers. My gaze flickers from him to the floor.

"It seemed like a terrible dream," he adds, his eyes blazing with a threat.

I get the sense that he was here, that he knows I had a nightmare because he was here, not from the camera. As much as I'd like to hide the sickening sense of defeat from my expression, I can't. He sees my weakness, and I can't hide from him.

"Answer me." His command comes out tense and deep.

I almost tell him, no, but then decide on silence, pretending to ignore how the fear that's growing inside of me makes my limbs feel numb. I expect anger from him, but all I can see is the twinkle of humor in his eyes.

"You will give me everything that I want," Cross says and then reaches out to me. My eyes close tightly as his fingers brush the hair from my face. He tucks the lock behind my ear and I think about biting him, about fighting him when I remember the first time he touched me so comfortingly, only to then grip my throat and hold me like his prized possession.

With another step forward, he bathes me in darkness, blocking the light and forcing me to push myself against the wall and stare up at him with genuine fear I wish I could deny.

"You're going to love doing it too," he whispers in the small space, heating the air between us and my body betrays me at the thought.

It makes no sense at all. Save the scent of his presence. He smells like the woods. Inhaling the deep scent reminds me of the way my mother used to describe our eyes. Like the canopy of the forest after a long day of rain. Maybe I could blame it on instinct.

Or maybe I'm just meant to be the whore to a monster.

I don't admit my response to him. There's no way in hell I ever would.

"Let me go," I whimper the plea and hate myself for it. I can pretend to be strong. He can't see what's deep inside of me. I can pretend to be stronger than he knows.

His only response is to chuckle, a deep and rough masculine sound that rumbles his chest and the anger I feel from it overwhelms me.

I'm barely holding on to my composure. I know if I strike him, he'll respond, and I will lose. I'm not stupid. *This is what he wants.* The realization makes my eyes widen. He's playing with his shiny new toy.

"Just kill me." My muscles scream as I stiffen them, refusing to lash out. Although my body heats and adrenaline pumps faster at the thought of him doing it, I still tell him to just get it over with. I don't want to be played with. "I'll never give you anything."

"Now what would that accomplish for me, songbird?"

I don't want to cry and give him the satisfaction. I refuse to. My eyes are already burning from being so fucking weak. I won't be weak. I won't let him win.

Be smart. A million possibilities run through my head at

what the smart choice would be in this moment, but the only situation I allow to rule my actions is to not give in. I'll wait. I'll survive day by day until my father comes. He will come. I know he will.

"I'll fight you until the day I die," I sneer at him with every ounce of conviction I can gather.

It only makes him smile. A wicked grin that sends a chill through my blood. "You'll find comfort in thinking that... for a little while." With a growing smile of triumph, he leaves me where I am. His shoes smack on the ground, and the sound grows quieter as he confidently strides to the door and turns the knob with ease.

How? He's simply walking away, and the door opens for him. I don't have time to consider anything. All I know at this moment is that the door is open. And whether or not he's there, I need to try to run. He opens the door just enough to get through. But I still run to it. I do my damnedest to make it to the door before it shuts and like the merciless prick he is, he leaves it open.

My bare heels bash against the cement as I sprint toward the light, but just as I make it, my hopes are so easily dashed. Just as the hope that I'll actually get out of here so easily burns into my chest, his tall broad frame fills the doorway, standing with a foreboding presence and taking a large step toward me.

A step so powerful and undeniably in control that I stagger backward, my foot scraping against the cement and throwing me off balance.

My ass hits the floor first and my head would have smacked against the concrete as well if Cross's hand wasn't wrapped firmly around my forearm. His fingers dig in and I let out a squeal of both surprise and pain.

"You're smarter than this," he hisses. The rage in his eyes swirls with darkness, but with it are golden flecks of intrigue and delight. "You won't leave this room until I say so."

I'm paralyzed by the certainty in his voice. The strength of his grip. The desire that drips from each of his words.

"You. Are. Mine. Aria." He says each word lower and lower until I can barely hear him over the pounding of my heart. The concept of being owned by this man is a deadly concoction that sends a ripple of both fear and desire straight to my core.

Without warning, he releases me, and I fall to the ground, still shaken but staring up at him. "I'm not an object to own. No one owns me!" I scream at him even though I don't believe my own words in this moment.

He merely smiles at me. As if it's all a joke to him.

"Let me go," I try to scream at him as if it's a demand, but the words are a pitiful plea even to my own ears.

Still, I try to stand, to get back up as he smiles and closes the door, leaving me right where he wants me.

I swear I hear him answer me before the steel door closes with finality. I would swear on my life I heard him say, "Never."

CHAPTER 9

CARTER

Daniel is my only brother who doesn't knock. He never has.

I know he isn't going to this time either. His steps are hurried, angered and I have to suppress a sigh of irritation. I'm fucking tired and I don't have time for his bullshit.

"This war between Talvery and the Romanos doesn't have anything to do with us."

Daniel's always had a knack for speaking as he enters the room, regardless of whether or not my gaze is down on my desk, focused on a spreadsheet of product and how much is selling. Having high demand is good, but some of this doesn't make sense. And it's only on the border of our territory that touches the Romanos' territory.

Pinching the bridge of my nose, I ignore him.

"Did you go to the club with Jase?" I ask Daniel as I continue down the order of supplies.

"Did you hear me?" Daniel questions me, kicking the office door shut and making his way across the office to sit in the chair opposite me.

"I did. You didn't tell me anything I don't already know." Shutting the laptop computer, I finally give him my attention and for a moment I'm caught off guard.

"You look like shit," I say, and I don't hide the surprise in my voice.

My brother's eyes spark with a hint of humor as he smirks at me and replies, "And you look like a fucking Ken doll. Drug dealer Barbie style."

A huff of a laugh escapes me as he runs his hand along the scruff on his jaw. "Addison isn't sleeping. She's having a hard time with this."

"With what?" I ask him, feeling a chill in my blood.

"With the shit that's going on. The war, not knowing who tried to take her or what they were planning."

"She doesn't need to know about a damn thing," I say beneath my breath with every bit of humor long gone. "You shouldn't have told her anything. We stay on lockdown. We wait for the Talverys and Romanos to trim their own numbers. If you have to tell her anything, that's all she should know."

Daniel's head tilts back slightly and he runs a hand down his face, his body slumped in the chair. "She's not allowed in the north wing and I don't want her leaving without me or someone else with her... and I'm not supposed to tell her anything?" he questions me, letting his chin drop and daring to look me in the eyes.

"The women should stay out of this." He fucking knows better.

"Says the man who started a war over a piece of ass."

"Careful." He cocks a brow at my response, but I stay firm.

Leaning forward, he puts both palms on the desk and asks quietly, like it's a secret, "What's going on with you?"

I steady my back against the leather chair, letting one hand fall to the armrest, my fingers tracing along the steel nail heads.

"I wish I knew," I tell him in a breath. "We have to move forward with this and there are some things that will benefit us, but it's a careful walk from here until the end."

Daniel nods his head, his eyes never leaving mine. "And when are we getting revenge on Marcus? The man who tried to take what's mine?"

"We don't know that it was Marcus who tried to take her."

"Who else would have done it?" Daniel asks but even as the last words slip out, his conviction wanes. Our enemies are surrounding us. The only saving grace is that they fear us, and they have other wars to fight.

"He has yet to answer any of our messages and no one's confirmed he had anything to do with it." Daniel's nostrils flare as he slams himself back into his seat, making the front legs of the chair nearly come off the floor while he looks past me and out the window.

"So, I'm supposed to do nothing and keep Addison in the dark?" Daniel asks with contempt. "I need to do *something*. I can't let him or whoever the fuck it was get away with it." His frustration is getting the better of him. And I understand. I do. But we have to be smart and know how best to move forward before we act.

"We don't know who did it. There will be nothing done until we do." My answer is absolute, with no room for negotiation, and the air tenses as Daniel considers me. A moment passes, and I can't breathe. My brothers are everything to me. All I have. And they've never questioned me. Not until this past week.

I'm losing my grip; I can feel it. And that's never a good thing.

Finally, he nods once and relaxes his posture, moving one ankle to rest on his knee.

"Can I ask you something else?" he asks, and I rest my elbow on the desk and then my chin in my hand, nodding as I do. He's going to ask me regardless.

"What are you doing with her?"

"It's personal." That short answer already reveals more than I've told anyone else, but Daniel shakes his head, a look of disappointment clearly written on his face.

"You aren't the brother I remember." He'll never know

the pain that comment causes me.

"Tell me what you remember, Daniel? You never saw anything past Addison." I practically hiss her name.

"What the fuck does that mean?" His anger is evident, and his jaw tightens.

"You had her and I had no one." My voice cracks at the revelation. Time marches on as we stare at each other. He has no idea how she saved him. Having someone to love, even if it is from a distance can give you hope. And hope is everything.

"We had each other," he finally tells me. I know he's thinking about the same shit I am. All the shit we went through. There were five of us, five brothers, but Daniel and I were the oldest and the two our father paid more attention to. If you can call what he did *attention*.

I let the anger and every other emotion fade, opening up the laptop to cue that this meeting is over. The truth slips by me unintentionally as I point out, "It's not the same."

"I just want to know you're not hurting her." He won't let it go. My grip tightens on the laptop as I try to remain calm.

"You have to trust me. Everything is about to change and if that girl had stayed where she was, she would have died." He waits for more. Proof, maybe. I don't know what he wants, but the less he knows, the better. "There's so much you don't know."

"You could tell me." There's a hint of sadness in his voice, or maybe I imagined it.

"Soon," I promise him. "Soon."

He doesn't say goodbye as he walks away. But as he makes it to the door, gripping the handle and swinging it open, I remember what he said about Addison. "Daniel. Give her this," I call out to him as I open the drawer. I have a few vials of S2L inside the small safe and toss one to him. He nods once and says something about Jase, but I don't hear, and he's already gone before I can question him.

Staring at the closed door, I think about how my brothers are the only constant I've had. Only them and no one else.

But admitting the truth out loud... I can't trust myself to do it.

The last time I admitted something of this weight, my world changed. I sparked the depraved monster inside of me to life and it changed everything.

The day Talvery left me to rot where he found me. I'll never forget the feeling as I heard my father's truck come to a stop. The old thing sputtered, and the sound was so comforting until his door shut and the anger in his voice was clear.

"What the fuck are you doing out in the open? Do you want someone to call the cops?" he yelled at me and when he tugged on my arm, the burns and cuts shot a horrible pain through my arm that made me scream in the dark alley. Bloodied and bruised, my father still tossed me around like I was nothing.

Couldn't he see what they'd done to me? I could hardly open my eyes.

"We'll get whoever did this, but come the fuck on before someone sees," he hissed between his teeth.

"They wanted to know who I worked for," I barely spoke as I hobbled to the car. Every bit of me hurt just to breathe. I slumped into the seat as he rounded the truck. And I know they saw. They had to have been watching me. Waiting to see who would come.

Country music played out as my father shut his door and took off down the street toward the dirt roads. I wanted to roll down my window so badly. I remember thinking I was dying, so I wanted to feel the wind on my face one last time. I'd coughed up so much blood, there was no way I'd be okay. My father ignored me as I asked him to do it, and instead, he turned down the music so only the sounds of the rumbling truck and his questions could be heard.

"Who's 'they?'" my father asked as he raced over a speed bump and my body jolted forward. I cried out like a bitch and he screamed the question again at me. It was fear in his voice though, not anger.

I know it now. Fear is what dictated his actions. Not strength like the man who'd done this to me.

"Talvery," I answered in a single painful breath. As I said his name, I remembered the look of Nicholas Talvery's freshly cleaned face only an inch from mine. I would never forget the way he looked at me like I was nothing and how much joy it brought him to know he could do whatever he wanted with me.

"What did you tell him?" he asked, and I looked at my father. I made sure to really look at him as I told him he was safe.

"I said I was just selling my dead mother's cancer meds. I said I was no one. And they believed me."

My heart has never hurt as much as it did at that moment when my father nodded his head and seemed to calm down. He was good at taking care of himself. He was good at living in fear.

That was the last day he looked at me as if I was a pawn in his game. My wounds were still fresh when I started hitting him back. And I never stopped. I wouldn't do the stupid shit he wanted me to. I would make money, a fuckton of it. But I never set foot on Talvery's turf again. I wasn't a dumb fuck like my father. And the next time he pushed me into the truck and screamed in my face so loud it shook my veins and the spittle hit my skin, I let my anger come forward, slamming my fist into his jaw.

I let the fear rule me in that moment. But it's the fear I saw in my father's eyes that defined the change between us.

Each time I went out, leading a life I didn't choose, I thought it would be my last. I wanted to die, and it wasn't the first time in my life that I wished for sweet death to end it all.

But without fear of death, I learned what power really was.

And none of my brothers understand that.

Not a single fucking one of them.

CHAPTER 10

ARIA

His eyes won't leave mine.

He won't leave the room.

He won't give me any space.

I don't know how many days I've been here, but I do know that today is different by the look in Cross's eyes.

It's hard to count the days. My eyes flicker to the carving of stripes on the wall just beyond Carter Cross's never-changing stern expression. Sitting on the metal chair a few feet from me puts him at the perfect height to block the etched stripes. One for each of the days I've been here. But I stopped a while ago.

My sleep is fucked and there aren't any windows in the room. I've noticed that when I lie down and curl up to sleep, the lights go off. Which means two things, as far as I can tell.

He wants me to sleep. And he doesn't want me to know how much time has passed. It could be midnight a week from when I was taken. Or it could be noon with even more days between now and my last day of freedom.

There are four stripes on the wall. One scrawled after each time I slept. But on the fifth day, I slept on and off with terrors of my childhood that woke me up constantly.

The first two days I got three meals, always delivered the same way. A small slot in the door opened, the food was shoved inside on a small foam tray and then the slot quickly shut with a deafening slam. I waited for hours by it on the third day, praying I could catch it, snatch the hand... I don't know what. All I knew was that on the other side was freedom. But I quickly found that the slot only opened when I was in the corner of the room farthest from the door. Otherwise, no food would come.

I can barely eat as it is, but hunger won a few times. And instantly, I slept afterward. I don't know if he drugged me or not, but the fear of sleeping is at war with the need to eat.

Either way, the food I'm given doesn't aid me in knowing what time of day it is. There doesn't seem to be a rhyme or reason as to what's on the tray.

There haven't been any breakfast foods at all. The last thing I ate was a biscuit and a chunk of ham. It was glazed with honey and my stomach was grateful. I devoured every scrap and then immediately regretted not eating whatever it was he'd given me before. If I don't eat what's given, he simply takes it away when I sleep. And somehow, he knows when I'm faking sleep. I tried that, too. I don't know how many times I laid in the darkness waiting for him to open the door, only to fool myself into sleeping and waking to the tray being gone.

So much wasted time.

Maybe losing the time is the first sign of victory for him.

But I want it back.

"What day is it?" I ask him and it's the first thing I've said in the time he's been in here.

He comes in every so often, merely watching me. Scooting his chair closer and waiting for something. I don't know what.

"It's Sunday."

Sunday... It was Thursday when I left to go to the bar. I know it was Thursday. "So, that means it's only been three days?" I ask him although inwardly my gut churns. It's not possible.

A devilish smile plays across his face.

"You slept a lot, songbird. It's been ten days."

His words steal the bit of courage from me and I turn to face the door rather than him, pulling my legs into my chest and sucking in a deep, calming breath. Ten days of screaming and crying in this room. Of not knowing when help is coming, or if it ever will. Of barely eating and only bathing from a bucket of water while hiding under my dirty clothes.

"If you would only kneel for me when I come in, I would give you so much more than this."

"Why are you doing this to me?" My question is a whispered breath. No tears come from my dry eyes and the pain in my chest is dull. There's only so much a person can take before they break. I don't need sleep or food even. I need answers.

"You ask that often," is his only response, as he straightens himself in the chair. Squaring his shoulders toward me and making the pressed dress shirt stretch tight across his shoulders.

His handsome features look like nothing but sin as he stares at me. I have to rip my eyes away from him. I can't look at him. He's a monster and that's the only thing I need to know about Carter Cross. A beautiful monster who enjoys depriving me and watching me fade into nothing.

"How about we play a game?" he asks me, and a chaotic laugh erupts from my lips.

"Come now, I promise you'll enjoy it," he says, and his voice is a promising caress.

"And what's the game, Cross?" I say his name out loud, staring defiantly into his eyes. I imagined his aggravation, maybe even anger at my response, but instead, he only grins at me. A crooked grin on a charming face. I wish I could smack it off.

"An answer for an answer," he says and that's when it

hits me.

"You think I know a thing about my father's business? You're wasting your time," I say but my voice betrays me as I speak. It cracks on my last words.

So, this is his plan? Steal me, lock me in a room with nothing for days until I'm desperate for change so he can get information from me? I know it's merely because I'm a woman. That's why they haven't tortured me. But it will come eventually, and I have nothing to give them.

My eyes burn with the need to cry, but I don't let it happen. "I swear to you," I barely get out and then stare into Cross's dark eyes, willing him to believe me, "I don't know anything."

"I know you don't." It takes a moment for me to register what he's said.

"Is this a trick?" I ask him, feeling as if I must be going crazy. The hope in my chest is fluttering so strongly. "I don't want to die," I whisper the confession.

"I'm not going to kill you." He answers simply, devoid of emotion, giving me nothing to hold on to other than the matter-of-fact words. "The Romanos would have killed you. You would have died or been captured and given a much crueler fate if I hadn't taken you first." I'm silent as I listen to him talk about me as if I'm merely a pawn to sacrifice. "Your best chance at surviving what's to come is with me."

Tears threaten to leak down my cheeks at the thought of men infiltrating my father's estate. At Nikolai being shot as he sits at the kitchen table where he always sits on the early weekend mornings. At my father being killed in the same room where my mother's life ended.

"Do you want to play the game?"

"I've never done well with games," I answer breathily, watching every inch of his expression for a hint at what's to come.

"The blanket is yours for playing," he says and nods toward a pile of fabric he'd tossed at my feet when he came in. And inwardly, I'm grateful. "Why don't you eat?" he asks me, and I know the game has started. An answer for an answer and he holds the first question.

Staring down at myself, I answer him with half honesty. "I'm not hungry." Ten days... I try to remember how many times I've eaten. Maybe six meals. At the realization, my stomach roils.

A moment passes before he shifts in the chair, leaning back but keeping his hands on his thighs. "If you lie, then I can lie," he says and the way he says the word "lie" forces me to stare into his eyes. It's like the devil himself discussing deceit. "That's the way this game works."

"I don't trust that you aren't going to drug me or poison me. Or something." The truth so easily pours from my lips.

My eyes drop to the ground at the reminder of all the horrific ideas that have flitted through my head since I've been here.

"It's only food and you need to eat." Again, there's no emotion, only a statement of fact. I watch him intently as he leans forward, resting his elbows on his knees and clasping his hands in front of him. "Your turn."

"What are you going to do with me?" I ask him without thinking twice.

"Feed you and keep you in here with nothing but what you have until you submit to me." He readjusts in the chair and adds, "You're a social creature and lonely. I can see how lonely you are." As he speaks to me, my gaze wanders and the hollow ache in my chest rises.

"I'm used to being lonely."

"I hear your prayers in the dark, songbird. I hear your wishes for someone to save you. Your father. Nikolai... Who is Nikolai?"

"A friend," I answer him, feeling the pain and agony sweep over my body. And feeling like a liar. The word friend sounds false even to my own ears, but it's been so long since Nikolai was anything else. And a friend is what he needed to be. Nothing more. Or else my father would have found out.

"Wrong answer. He is no one anymore. They're all gone, and no one is coming to save you."

"Gone?" The word comes out like a question, but the monster in front of me doesn't answer. My eyes close as I inhale deeply, thinking he's lying. They're coming. They'll come for me.

"You're bored, alone, and starving yourself into nothing. You will submit to me, or you will stay like this forever."

My lips kick up into a small smile I can't contain, and I don't know why. I must be going crazy.

"You think that's funny?" A hint of anger greets his words and it only makes my smile grow, but it's accompanied with tears leaking from the corner of my eyes. And I don't even know when I started crying.

Shaking my head, I brush away the tears from just under my eyes. "It's not funny, no. And now it's your turn." He's going to keep me here like this? He could keep me here forever.

Even as I think the statement, the overwhelming loneliness consumes me. I have nothing and this prison is eating my sanity alive. Hours pass where I simply stare at the wall, praying it will offer me something different than the day before.

He watches me as I sway from side to side slightly.

"What does submit mean?" I talk over him just as he starts to speak. My words are harsher than I thought they'd be and he cocks his brow, not answering me and then asks his question.

Rules of the game, I suppose.

"What is your favorite food?"

Dizziness overwhelms me for a moment and I rest my head against the wall. He's going to win this game. And all the others. He's cheating and I'm deteriorating.

"Bacon, I guess. Everyone loves bacon," I answer halfheartedly, partly because I'm tired of this game already and partly because I need a little humor in this situation. "There's this sandwich from the corner store by my house. My mother used to take me there." I stare at the ceiling while I talk, not really to him, but just to talk and think about something other than this. Although it's nice to have someone around. I feel an empty hollowness inside of me. I'd rather that than the sickening feeling of defeat.

Licking my lower lip, I continue. "She took me there every weekend. Coffee and pastries for her, but they had this sandwich I loved, and they still have it. It's turkey and bacon with ranch dressing on a pretzel roll." My head lolls to the side and I glance at Cross, whose usual stern expression has been replaced by a look of curiosity. "I think that may be my favorite."

The memory of my mother makes me smile and I almost tell him more. I almost tell him about the day she died and how we went there first. But she didn't get her usual pastries or coffee, and we didn't stay long. I was so upset that she didn't get me my sandwich, but she promised we'd get it tomorrow.

If I hadn't been so young and foolish, I would have known what was happening. How my mother was running from someone she'd spotted. How she ran home for protection, only to find the monster was already there.

God, I miss her. I miss anyone and everyone. I hadn't realized how lonely I'd become.

"Would you like to go home when this is over?" Cross's

question distracts me from the thoughts of the past.

"When it's over?" I ask for clarification and I only receive a nod from him.

A deal with the devil. It's all I can think. The war doesn't matter, even if that's what he's hinting at. He'll keep me however long he wants, regardless of what he tells me now.

"You already know the answer to that." They're the only words I give him. It's my turn once more, so I ask him again, "What do I have to do to leave?"

"There is no leaving unless I want you to leave."

"Then why I am here?" The desperation is evident.

"I've already told you. I want you to submit to me. To desire my touch and earn it by kneeling and waiting to obey me. To be mine, in every way."

"You know that would never happen," I say absently. "I'll stay in this room forever or wait for something else to happen. I have nothing but time."

"I'm going to make a change to your routine," Cross says as if it's a threat.

Again, my head falls to the side to look at him, my energy waning. "Is that so?" I ask him, and he quirks a devious grin.

"You'll only eat when I feed you. Bite by bite." His eyes flicker with a heat that should scare me, but it does other things to me that I choose to ignore. "You should have eaten before, songbird. Your defiance is only hurting you."

The thought of him feeding me is something that will

haunt me for hours once he's gone, I already know it. It's not just the loneliness that attracts me to Cross. I felt it the moment I saw him.

"I wasn't going to eat anyway," I tell him in a single breath rather than allowing my imagination to get the best of me. I've heard death by starvation is a horrible way to die and I know I'll have to figure out another way. I know I'll cave, just like I already have. As if reading my mind or maybe knowing better, Cross smirks at me, but it's different from the previous ones. There's something almost melancholy about this one.

"You'll eat," he tells me and then stands up without another word. As he turns the doorknob, I close my eyes knowing the bright light is coming. Even with my eyes closed, I can see it. And then it's gone, and once again I'm alone and trapped in the room.

I should feel a touch of ease, knowing he's given me some information I can hold on to. But all I can think about is my mother and the last day I saw her.

She wanted to leave and run away. She begged me to understand. And I cried when she told me, "*Ria, please.*"

I'll never forget the wretched way my name fell from her lips that day. The fatal flaw of any mother is how much her love for her children will blind her. It's my fault. Fresh tears leak down my face and I don't even bother wiping them away as I crawl to the mattress.

It takes a bit longer than usual for him to do it, but with

the blanket wrapped tightly around me, the lights in the room go off. Loneliness is my only companion unless I give in to the memories. And I hadn't realized how harmful they can be. My own past is becoming my enemy.

I find myself filled with nothing but regret as sleep takes over.

If only I could go back and not fight her.

If only I could go back and tell her, we can't go home.

CHAPTER 11

CARTER

It's different when I'm in the cell with her. When there's nothing but an isolated war between the two of us. I know she'll break, and she'll love it when she does.

When I'm in there with her, staring her down and watching every small, calculated movement from her, all I feel is the need to bring her to that edge and watch her fall.

I can picture her beautiful hair a tangled mess as I fist it in my hand, taking my pleasure from her even if she'd give it freely. She'll be on her knees, desiring the same things that I do.

It consumes me when the four walls of the cell surround me, but the moment the steel door closes behind me with a finality that another day has passed where I don't have control of her, the desire changes to desperation.

She *has* to submit. To kneel when I walk into her cell and to wait eagerly for my command.

And soon.

I have other plans and I want her to be a part of them. She needs to give in. It starts with a simple kneel.

I'm still reeling from seeing her sweet defiance when the door shuts tight. Slipping the painting back into place, I get a glimpse of my brother as he walks toward me in the hall.

"You're waiting for me?" I ask him, and he matches my pace as we head toward my office.

"I think I know why it's hitting heavier on the edge of the south side, closer to the Romanos." He doesn't waste a second to start talking business.

"The supply?" I ask him for clarification. The drug market is predictable. That's the best part about an addiction. It's steady, rampant, and easily maintained. When demand increases in only one area, there's a reason for it. And I need to know why this shift is so unexpected.

"Romanos have their hands on it. They have to be producing it by the amount they're selling." My blood chills in response to Jase's revelation. My jaw tenses as we make our way down the stairs. Each step only emphasizes the hollow pounding in my ears.

He wanted an ally.

He wanted to do business together.

He's nothing but a liar, a thief, and a spineless prick.

But none of that is news to me.

"He's selling S2L?" I ask him. "Are you sure?" The drug is ours. Ours alone. It was only a matter of time before everyone else wanted it, but instead of getting the details, Romano stole it. The stupid fuck.

"I'm positive," Jase answers me and I imagine Romano's ugly snarl of a smile as I punch his teeth in. I can practically feel the way the tight skin of my knuckles would split as his teeth broke under them. "I got a sample from their streets, took it back and it's definitely our mix. A heavier version than what we got off Malcolm."

"Do you think Romano knows why the pharmacy pulled it and the side effects?" I ask Jase as I push my office door open.

We acquired a banned drug, manipulated it, and just started selling S2L, street name Sweet Lullaby. It was designed to help with anxiety and insomnia. It can aid in weaning off an addiction to harder drugs. But S2L is the most addictive because of the way it calms you, assures you and your entire being that everything is just as it should be and lull you into a deep sleep. Thus, the name, Sweet Lullaby. The undesired side effects were too great to risk... for them. Not for us.

"I think they know exactly what it is," he says with a touch of anger, "seeing as how they fucked with the formula." The door practically slams shut from the weight of his push. He doesn't look me in the eyes until he's seated in the chair opposite mine. It's only when he says the next sentence that I finally fall into mine. "They made it more potent. It's practically lethal with the way it numbs the senses, slowing the heart and forcing the body into a deep sleep."

My thumb brushes against my jawline as I consider what Romano is up to. "He stole our drug; he's selling a version that's deadly on his territory..." I think out loud, not bothering to hide my string of thoughts from Jase.

Jase is the one who got a hold of the drug from an asshole who owed us a debt but had secrets within the industry. Malcolm was useful enough that we let him live. For a little while.

"He's selling on his territory. Sweet Lullaby but the lethal version is going by ST, Sweet Tragedy. He must not have enough, or else we wouldn't see the increase in demand."

"The thing about demand is that those who are addicted are still living."

"Unless it's being used on someone else."

"So, he's selling it as a weapon? Not as a drug?" I have to admit the thought occurred to us as well, but until we have a preventative drug that renders the deadly version useless, I wouldn't dare to even hint at the possibility.

His fingers tap, tap, tap with a nervousness on the armrest. "The thing that doesn't fit though... What doesn't add up... is that there isn't a rise in the death toll. There's no sudden spike in murders or people dying in their sleep."

"They're either buying and not using, or they're selling it elsewhere. Maybe overseas?"

"I think the Romanos aren't keeping up with the production of S2L, they have a small demand, but word got out that we're the suppliers. So, Romano decided to up the ante, make the potent version which got someone's attention. Someone who wants control of the market. Whoever it is, he's buying every drop he can of the potent version, and every bit of ours so he can make the change himself, concentrating it and making an untraceable weapon."

"How could Romano be so fucking stupid?" The words are pushed through my clenched teeth. We sold the drug as a relaxer, a way to ease pain and keep people from ODing on the deadlier shit. It's the perfect way to make an addiction last. And Romano's greed had to fuck it up.

I'm silent as I consider Jase's theory.

"Whoever's gathering it is on his side, not ours. Someone who wants his territory, maybe?" he suggests, and I can only nod in response. Whoever it is isn't doing a good job of hiding their whereabouts and intentions. Unless of course, they wanted it to be known. My thumb brushes along my chin again as I consider every asshole I know who could want Romano's place. Maybe they wanted us to know.

"I want Mick's crew on the south side, tracking the information of every buyer and to find a connection. I want to know who's fucking with it and if they're selling anywhere else."

"It's expensive shit, this potent version. And whoever is buying in bulk has to be waiting to resell."

"Maybe they think Romano will lose the war, and they'll come in to a territory with a built-in high demand, already supplied with the drug?"

Jase nods at my prediction, clucking his tongue and still tapping his finger on the chair. "That's not a problem for us," he adds.

"You think they'd stop at the Romanos?" I question him and like the intelligent fucker he is, he shakes his head, the small grin ticking up his lips. Jase loves a challenge. He lives to snuff out those who think they can threaten what we've worked so fucking hard to build.

"So, we don't tell Romano?" he asks me.

"Not a word. He stole from us." I look him dead in the eye as I come to the conclusion with my brother.

"You still want to do the dinner next week?" he questions me.

Romano thinks it's a celebratory dinner.

Talvery is weak. It's almost a letdown at how easily everything is crumbling around him. There's already a crack within his own factions, or so says the word on the street. Half his crew is taking bribes from Romano. I'm reluctant to let my guard down. Looks from the outside can be deceiving. I know that all too well.

Nonetheless, Romano will come here to this celebratory dinner. And I'll have the utmost enthusiasm as his host and partner in celebrating the fall of his longtime rival. Long enough to lure him in at least.

"Yes." I can't stress my words enough as I stare at the box under the bookshelf on the right side of the room. "Next week he'll be here, at our table, in our home."

"It's not about the war or the drug though, is it?" Jase's question brings my gaze back to him. "It's about her?"

His intuition freezes my blood. I have to remind myself that he's my brother, that he would know because he's been so close for so long. I have to remind myself that there isn't a way another soul could even begin to guess the truth.

"Yes," I reply cautiously as our eyes lock and I wait for his reaction. Once again, I fall prey to the ticking of the clock as he carefully chooses his words. "She's part of it."

"We could give her money and let her run," he offers. And he assumes wrong.

"She'll run right back to her father, and you know it."

"Then let her," Jase says and shrugs as if it's no concern to us if she were to retreat back to her father.

"And have the Romanos and everyone else think we're so weak that we just let a girl walk away?"

"Since when did you start caring what they think?" he asks me, still feigning that this conversation is a casual discussion that means nothing.

"They need to *think* that I don't care what they think. But how they see us matters more than anything. For us to control what they do, we have to know what they think. We have to be able to manipulate it for us to know what they'll do next."

"You can say you grew tired of her." Jase continues to make suggestions and this time it spikes my anger. I've grown tired of him pushing me to let her go, to eliminate her from the equation. She's too valuable to me.

"Never," I answer in a single breath without thinking.

"Never?" Jase asks questioningly, only now dropping his guard, his grip tightening on the leather armrest and letting an inkling of anger show.

"I wanted her... before."

"Before Romano offered her?" Jase's interest is piqued.

I only nod in response, feeling the confession so close to coming to life.

"Why?" he asks me, and I don't answer him. I can't. Instead, I offer him a small truth. "He didn't offer her. I told him it would be her or no one," I say softly, to ensure the words will vanish by the time he can hear them.

"What are you going to do to her?" he asks me again. My brothers keep asking me that and it only pisses me off.

"She has to fear me... for a while." My thumb nervously runs along my bottom lip. "It won't always be like this."

"You need to give me more," he demands, and I quickly spit back, "I don't need to give you shit."

A beat passes and the rage slips into my blood. The memories and everything I've worked for, everything we've become turns to hate and ruin.

"This conversation is over," I tell him. He only smiles. A coy knowing smile, and nods. The tension evaporates and without another word, he leaves the office. Although I know he's left with far more than he gave.

As I watch him leave, the ticking of the clock won't stop. Tick tock. Tick tock. Tick tock. My gaze moves from the box to the laptop with a black screen staring back at me.

Deep breaths. In and out. Deep breaths bring me back to her.

When I flick the monitors back to life, to see what my little songbird is doing, she's already asleep.

It's been so long since these memories have haunted me, but they come back slowly as I turn off the lights in her cell.

Memories that made me. Memories she's a part of, even if she doesn't know.

The memory of the day I learned who Talvery was and what fear could really do to a person.

There comes a point when it doesn't matter what the last punch broke or how much blood you've lost. It's a point where you can't feel anything anymore.

Your vision is blurry, and you know death is so close that you pray for it. It's the only thing that will take it all away.

Nothing makes sense. Even as my head snaps back and more warmth bubbles from my mouth, the pain is nothing. And knowing the end is near, it provides a comfort. The chains holding me to the chair fade away and I can hardly feel them digging into my skin.

But even in all of that, she meant something. I knew it instantly. She had the strength to destroy the hope that it would all end soon.

Her small fists banged on the door that was so close but so far away.

Her voice called out and broke through the fog of reality.

I couldn't hear what she screamed, but it was something so urgent, her father put down the wrench. I remember the heavy metallic sound of it falling onto the floor mixing with her sweet feminine pleas for him to help her through the closed door.

I was so close to everything being over, and she saved me. Even if she doesn't remember it. She never even saw me.

It took years before I let myself think of her again. And of that day.

I almost had an out. I was so close to leaving this life a good soul. Maybe not pure, not perfect, but a better man than I am now and an innocent soul.

She's the reason I lived and turned into this.

I don't just want her at my mercy.

I want everything she has.

I'm not going to stop until I have her and her everything.

CHAPTER 12

ARIA

I think it's been two days since Cross changed the rules. If I'm right, it's been almost two weeks since I've been here. And two full days of not eating anything.

I refuse to eat from his fingers like a dog. I'm not his pet. The way he looks at me like he'd wish for nothing more than for me to kneel between his legs and accept each morsel is riddled with both desire for me and desire for power over me. The combination is heady, and it plays tricks with my mind. I'm addicted to the hunger in his eyes but I'm afraid of what's to come if I give in.

I don't want to submit and kneel in front of him. At least, that's what I keep telling myself. Each ache I have reminds myself of this. As the loneliness stretches and the boredom makes me wonder if I'm going crazy, I have to remind myself. It's always a reminder.

The thoughts make my breathing heavy and my stomach rumble. The sickening part of all of this is that I'm looking forward to him opening the door. I want him to come in tonight like he did last night and the night before. With a silver platter of temptation.

I'm starving and I know I have to give in. I know I will at some point. He's right. I will eat. I'm already praying for him to open the door, even as I curse him and clench my hands into fists, swearing I'll be strong enough to refuse him.

He's going to win. I can feel it.

I'm praying for him to come, so I can have something to eat. Whatever he brings, if he were to come right now, I'd accept. No matter how much I wish it weren't true. I would do anything to eat right now. To eat anything at all.

My eyes lift from the ground to the door as it creaks open. I don't lift my head and I stay on the dirty ground, stiff and unmoving.

I can feel his eyes on me, but I can't look at him. The only thing that holds my attention is the tray balanced in his right hand and held at his chest. I can't see what's on it yet, but I can smell it.

My eyes close slowly and I nearly groan from the sugary scents that flood my lungs. When I finally open my eyes, cued by the sound of him moving the chair across the floor and closer to me, I see it all. I see the tasty treats that will be responsible for my pathetic undoing.

The tray is full of the sweetest things. Berries and chunks of mango and fresh pineapple.

It's all brightly colored and arranged beautifully. Like I said, a silver platter of temptation.

"How's your hand?" Cross asks me and it's only then that I even acknowledge him.

"Fine." My short answer is rewarded with him pulling the tray closer into his lap. "I think it's bruised," I offer him in an attempt to give him what he wants.

"You were banging your fist on that door for over forty minutes." My teeth grit at his response.

"Well, you heard me at least," I say, although I can't deny that it hurts. I'm so fucking alone. And tired and sore and aching with pains. But so alone more than anything else.

"I did," is all he says.

There's a routine that comes with Carter Cross. He likes things to be done a certain way, maybe so that it can appear that he's predictable but I'd much sooner think it's so he can force my own behavior to be predictable for him.

In these sessions, the ones where food is offered, he attempts the semblance of a conversation before offering food. And today, I know I'll talk back. I know I'll do what he wants. I'm that desperate.

"You're dirty," he tells me with what seems like sincere

sympathy. "You don't wash yourself like I'd hoped you would."

I bite my tongue at the perverted comments, but I can't hold it all in. "I'm not a dog to be bathed." I can't hide the anger. I should fake my tone like he does, but I choose not to. He'll feed me regardless. I hope. He only smiles at me in response and it nearly makes me back away from him. Not because of the way he's looking at me, but because of how my body reacts to the smile. How he seems to enjoy it when I don't hold back. It's dangerous. *He's* dangerous.

"You're tired."

"It's difficult to sleep on the floor." Even as I answer him, I can feel how heavy the bags are under my eyes.

"There's a mattress at least," he quips, and those piercing eyes stare deeper into me like he can see through the wall of defense. Just the way he looks at me makes me question everything.

Time evades me as I stare back at him, feeling those same walls crumble deep inside of me. I try to suppress the hate I have for him in this moment, just so I can get this over with and eat.

"You look weak, songbird."

"You keep calling me that," I bite back.

"I've never called you weak," he says, and his answer is just as stern as mine.

"I meant 'songbird.' You keep calling me songbird." My voice cracks. I don't want him to call me anything. Not my name, not a sweet nickname. It doesn't reflect how he truly sees me. It's meant to weaken me, make me soften. "Stop calling me that."

"No," he says in a hardened voice. "Now come here, songbird Come kneel in front of me and let me feed you."

This is the second part of his routine and the one where I've told him to go fuck himself over and over again. But today, I slowly move my body and get on my hands and knees. I swallow my pride and it hurts. It physically hurts. I didn't know pride was a spiked ball until I move one knee in front of the other. My body is hot with embarrassment and shame as I stop at his feet.

I can't open my eyes until his rough hand brushes against my jaw. I wish I didn't feel the need to lean into him. Loneliness consumes me every day. If I could pause this moment and pretend I'm somewhere else, with someone else, I'd lean into his strong touch. I'd allow myself to enjoy his warmth and comfort.

But as it is, I'm staring into the dark eyes of a man who's held me like this before. And then so quickly shown how easily he could hurt me.

Swallowing thickly, I wait for the third part. Only seconds until he tells me to open my mouth.

As if reading my mind, Cross lets his thumb brush along the seam of my lips. It's a gentle caress that ignites something primitive in me, heating my core and making my heart beat furiously inside my chest. My knees inch forward, obeying the command from my body to move closer to him.

Closer to the man who controls my freedom. Closer to the gentle touch.

"Open," he commands me, and I feel my lips part of their own accord.

My eyes stay closed until his hand moves away, and his warmth is replaced with the chill of the air in the cell.

My heart flickers with fear until I watch him pick up a chunk of strawberry and lift it to my lips. I'd be ashamed at how greedily I eat the small piece of fruit if only consuming it didn't make me feel as though I'm starved. The sweetness falls into a pit of hollow hunger pains. And again, my body moves closer to him.

He doesn't say anything or hint at anything other than his desire to keep feeding me. And I accept every piece with a hunger that only seems to intensify. My hands find their way to his knees, gripping him as I swallow the next piece he's offering me.

It takes me far too long to realize I'm touching him. His groan of approval is what cues my awareness, but as I try to pull away, he does the same to the fruit in his grasp.

"Stay." He gives me the simple command, and so I do. I cling to him for more.

The part that's truly shameful though is how much hearing him tell me to stay made me crave more of him. His hand on mine, watching him watch me.

A moment passes where I realize he knows my forbidden thoughts.

My greatest fear is that he'll voice them and bring them to life. I force my fingers to dig deeper into his leg and I open my lips wider, silently begging for more, so I can hide the temptation that grows hotter between us.

I think he's doing it slowly on purpose. Picking up the bits of sweet fruit and taking his time before he slips them between my lips.

"Open wider," he commands me and it's only because my stomach pains with the need to eat that I obey him, that's what I tell myself. I close my eyes, holding back every other thought.

"Look at me," he commands as I swallow the small morsel and his strong hand cups my chin, forcing my head up. The juice from his fingers wets the underside of my chin in his grasp. He's so close, his dark eyes swirling with an intensity that holds my gaze captive. "You're so strong," he tells me, and I hate him for it. "You don't believe me, but you are."

The rough pad of his thumb brushes against my bottom lip and I almost bite him, just to spite him. To prove to him that whatever he assumes I'm thinking is all in his head. I catch the broad smile growing on his face as I look back up at him.

He offers me another piece and I take it in my mouth. I have to wait for him to pull his fingers away, but he doesn't.

My gaze moves back to his and he lowers his lips to my

neck, his fingers still in my mouth and the juice of the fruit tasting even sweeter. His short stubble brushes my collarbone and then he whispers in my ear, "See how strong? You'd love to bite me, but you know how to survive."

His hot breath tickles my neck and sends goosebumps down my body. Shamefully, my nipples harden and my back bows slightly. "Such a good girl, Aria," Cross says, and I pull away from him, leaving the fruit between his fingers and brushing my ass against the cement as I scoot backward, putting distance between us.

The fear is alive within me, but it's changed. I fear what I'm capable of and how much I'd enjoy it.

The vision of him pinning me down on the ground flashes before my eyes and cruelly, it only makes me hotter. I swallow thickly, feeling my cheeks heat with a blush.

Cross doesn't move from his chair. "You're all done?" he asks me. I can't look him in the eye. I don't even trust myself to speak. Maybe this is what it's truly like to be broken.

"Is it because you've finished, or because you're wet for me?" he asks me in a husky voice that only adds to my desire for him.

"Fuck you," I say beneath my breath, narrowing my eyes and letting my blunt nails dig into the cement.

Cross lets the trace of a smile play on his lips, but it doesn't reach his eyes as he stands up, towering over me. "I told you I wanted you, Aria. And I get everything I want. Just remember that."

CHAPTER 13

CARTER

She hasn't eaten, she's barely moved since she gave in last night. I've come in twice since then and both times she's denied me even though in three days all she's eaten is a handful of fruit.

I can feel the tension between us. I know she's at war with it as much as I am. But she spends her nights screaming and barely sleeping. The little bit of progress during the day is erased and there's nothing I can do about it.

She's going to cave again and I can feel it on the horizon. I've never been so eager to come into this cell as I am today.

I have to hide my smile as she slinks from the mattress to the floor. She never stays on the mattress when I come in. At least, she hasn't yet.

My heart beats hard as I watch her expression fall.

There's no tray tonight. No offering for her.

It's easy to see her breathing pick up as she registers I'm here for something else.

I intentionally let the chair drag along the floor as I make my way to her.

"I don't have anything to say," she tells me as I sit down only a few feet away from her. Far enough so that she can crawl to me and kneel. The crawling part I'm not interested in. She decided to do that on her own, but I don't care how I get her on her knees in front of me. So long as she submits.

"That's interesting that you would start the conversation then, isn't it?" She doesn't respond. Her collarbone looks more prominent today than it ever has. I couldn't see it on the monitors, but three days of barely eating is starting to show and I don't like it. Starved is not how I want her.

I should feel remorse, not anger at the observation.

"Why make it harder on yourself?" I question her with a deep tone of disapproval.

And once again, she doesn't answer.

"You'll cave again. You can't help yourself. You realize that, don't you?" She's a smart girl. Anyone with any bit of intelligence knows that starvation is painful, and the instinct to survive will kick in over pride.

"Just let me go," she says weakly, brushing under her eyes and hiding the tears. So close to breaking. So, fucking close.

"I'm getting tired of hearing you make that request."

"Then both of us are tired," she says softly, picking at her dirty clothes. I would give her everything if only she'd obey me.

"You wanted me," I remind her, and she huffs a pathetic sound of disgust.

Her eyes narrow as she looks me in the eyes and tells me, "You aren't what I want."

"What did you want then?" I ask her, leaning forward in my seat so quickly that I startle her. I'm only inches away and so close I can feel the heat from her body. She turns away from me, looking toward nothingness on the blank wall.

"Answer me," I say and there's little patience in my voice. My body tenses as I move forward in my seat so I'm as close to her as I can be. I don't like what she does to me, but even more, I don't like that I don't know what to do with her. I don't want her like this. I need her to break now, her mind before her body.

She looks at me with a stare of contempt before barely speaking the words, "I don't know what I wanted."

"You wanted me to fuck you," I tell her in a voice intended to be seductive. I practically whisper. "I'd feed you, care for you, fuck you and put you to bed used and sated." She's silent as I move back to a relaxed position in the uncomfortable chair. "That's what you wanted."

"I just wanted my fucking notebook back!" she screams at me with a bite of anger I know must've hurt. Swallowing thickly, she looks away from me as her eyes turn glossy.

My heart pounds hard, just once, then stops for a moment as she wipes her eyes.

"You want a notebook?" I ask her, although I don't know what the fuck she's talking about.

Her chest rises and falls steadily as she looks at me. Each breath deepening the dip in her collarbone. "Tell me," I command her.

"My drawing pad," she murmurs softly, anger and contempt forgotten. "That's what led me to the bar where those assholes got me," she whispers with defeat. "I just wanted my drawing pad back."

"A specific one?" I ask as my brow raises slightly. It's not going to happen. I can get her a new one, but I'm not risking what's already been set in motion to find something she's left behind.

"Yes," she whispers and parts her lips to tell me something else, but I can't and won't hunt down any of her possessions.

"It's gone," I say flatly, cutting off her words.

I watch as she swallows and note the way the sadness returns to her eyes. "Any would do." Her eyes search my face warily as she sits back against the bed, making it dip with her weight. She's frail with a look of submission brimming close to the surface.

"A drawing pad. What else do you want?" My fingers itch to trace along her jaw and force her to look at me. To force her to make this easier on herself and both of us.

She peeks up at me through only slits, her dark lashes barely letting me see any of her eyes. But in the small bit she offers me, I see nothing but rage.

"You have something to say?"

"Fuck you," she spits.

I've never felt the urge to kiss her until now. In filthy clothes and all. It's quiet between us as I imagine gripping the nape of her neck and taking her lips with mine. She'd bite me. I know she would because she thinks she should, and that only makes me harder.

"That mouth of yours. That's what's going to get you into trouble."

"As if I'm not in trouble already," she answers me through clenched teeth, lifting her chin at me.

"You will be if you don't obey me." Each word comes out heavy, making my chest clench with a tightness of what's to come. My breathing is shallow, and my blood burns a little hotter.

I can see her lips twitch with the need to speak, but she bites her tongue.

This is the version of Aria that I want. The raw anger of knowing and accepting that she's at my mercy.

"Tell me what you really think, Aria," I say softly although the words ring out loudly in my ears. My gaze is locked on hers. My blood rushing in my ears. All I can do is wait for her.

One beat. Two beats of my heart before she whispers in a cracked voice, "You're a monster."

"And why is that?"

"Because of what you want from me," she says quiety, but she doesn't break eye contact.

"What is it that I want from you?" I ask her as I grip the edge of the chair tighter.

"You want to fuck me." She doesn't hesitate to answer but the anger in her expression morphs to pain as she rips her gaze away from mine.

"Of course, I want to fuck you," I tell her in as calm a voice as I can manage. My gaze slips down to her curves and I have to force them back up to see her doe eyes back on mine as she scoots farther back on the bed. She's searching for comfort and safety, but all she's doing is making me want to pursue her.

I lean forward, resting my elbows on my knees. "The second I saw you, I wanted you." My confession comes out a whisper and the memory of her weeks after that night happened years ago flashes through my mind. I had to know the face of the angel who'd saved me. If only she had known then what she was doing, if only she'd known I wasn't worth saving. The hate and love I've had for her has warred for years within me.

Silence separates us for a moment. And then another.

"Just get it over with," she breathes the words but doesn't look up. The tone of defeat rings false.

"Is that because you want me too, but you don't have the courage to admit it?" I dare to challenge her and again that anger comes back full force.

"Fuck. You." She leans forward as she says each word, practically spitting them. And the rage and defiance only make my cock more eager to thrust deep inside of her.

"You will, little songbird." Lust pumps through my blood as she inches back on the bed yet again, her gaze fixed next to me as if she's watching my every move but doesn't want me to know it.

That only makes the hint of a smirk on my lips grow.

The chair scoots back as I stand and the sound of it scratching the floor frightens Aria. She sits up a little straighter, a little stiffer and watches me with wide eyes as I take two steps closer to her.

"You want to get it over with?" I ask her as I reach for my belt. I want her to see how hard I am for her. And teach her a lesson.

My belt slips through the loops of my pants, leaving the sound of leather brushing against the fabric to sing in the air. My blood is laced with adrenaline and lust as I watch her breathe heavier and faster.

The metal of the buckle clinks on the ground as it lands and then I unzip my pants. A flush travels up Aria's chest and into her cheeks.

"Come here," I give her the small command with the bit

of breath left in my lungs as I grip my thick erection through my pants and she watches. I swear her lips part and her thighs clench as she watches.

Her wide eyes dart from my cock to my eyes.

"Come here," I tell her again when she doesn't move. I know she wants me. Maybe not like this, but I have to show her what power she has. Until she submits, all she has is power over me. "Get down on your knees in front of me," I add and palm myself again. "Aria." Her name comes out hard on my lips, but dripping with sin and desire as I add, "I fucking want you."

I don't miss the small gasp from her lips as she hesitates another second.

I watch every small change in her expression. From how her nails dig into the mattress, to how her body tenses and makes the bed creak as she inches forward as if she's going to listen to me. She swallows so loudly I can hear it as she slowly climbs off the bed. She stands on weak legs before dropping slowly in front of me, down onto her knees.

My pulse quickens but I don't know how. All the blood in my body feels like it's in my dick.

"If I leaned down and shoved my hand between your thighs," I ask her, holding back a groan from the thought, "how wet and hot would your cunt feel right now?"

Her eyes widen, and she leans back, but with the way she's seated, with her knees under her, she can't lean back far without being off balance.

"Do you know what it will feel like when I finally shove myself deep inside your tight little cunt?" I ask as my dick pulses with need and I have to stroke it once more.

She breathes out heavily, nearly violently and avoids my gaze.

"You're going to scream my name like your life depends on my mercy." I stroke myself again and again. Fuck, I'm so eager for her touch my dick is throbbing so hard it hurts. "I won't show you mercy, Aria, I'm going to fuck you like you're mine to ruin."

She whimpers and struggles to remain still in front of me. Her thighs clench as I kick the chair behind me, so I can crouch down in front of her.

Her hazel eyes are wide and filled with desire.

"I want to give you everything," I whisper as I lean forward, letting my lips trail along her jaw. A ripple of unease runs through me as I realize the truth in those words.

She shivers, and I watch her nails dig into her thighs. "You have to tell me what you want, and when I ask you how badly you want my cock, you better tell me the truth."

I pull away, letting my fingers trace down the right side of her face, and then lower, to her neck and collarbone. Then lower to her chest. "I want to see how you react when I pinch and bite these," I tell her as my fingers travel to the peaks of her breasts.

"Do you think you'll enjoy it?" I ask her. And for the first time, she admits a small truth, nodding her head once and then ripping her eyes from me.

Her breathing is chaotic, and I know she's ashamed.

"I desperately want to feel you cum on my cock," I admit to her, whispering in her ear since she still has her head turned. "Tell me what you want."

All I can hear is our tense breathing mix in the hot air between us.

"Tell me, songbird," I say, willing her to give in.

Time seems to stretch on forever.

"A drawing pad." Blinking away the haze in her eyes and still denying what she truly wants, she utters useless words.

And I leave her just like that, wanting and panting and flushed with need.

She'll learn to ask for what she wants. Or she'll stay here forever.

CHAPTER 14

ARIA

I've never felt like this before.

Like there's nothing left of me but a shell of a weak and pathetic person. I'm on the edge of loathing myself and the way my body begs me to give in to Cross.

But most of all, I pity myself and that's what's driving the hate.

My father isn't coming. Nikolai isn't coming.

I was worried that they were dead, but Carter told me yesterday that they're still alive and the war is only getting started. I don't know if he's lying to me or not. If he wanted to offer me hope so he could crush it. I don't know anything anymore and nothing gives me hope of getting out of here.

Even as the thought hits me, I crumple forward and

bury my face in my grimy hands. They smell of dirt but as I struggle to breathe and maintain any sense of composure, I don't give a damn. No matter how many times I bathe myself with the warm water that waits for me when I wake up, I feel dirty. The kind of dirty that doesn't wash away.

I'm alone. A prisoner. And I don't see any way out of here. There's no white knight planning on barging in here. I'm not worth it. If I was, they would find me, they would come for me. They would save me and make Cross pay for keeping me here to starve and torment with thoughts of being his fuck toy.

Fate sent a dark knight after me instead. With dinged and scratched armor and a taste for something that I shouldn't crave. My face is too hot when I pull my hands away, calming my breath and leaning my head against the wall behind me.

Exhaustion has taken over and I know it's because I don't eat.

But I could, a little voice whispers in the crevices of my mind. The same dark corners where the memories of yesterday send a warmth through my body.

My teeth dig into my lip as I remember how his skin felt against mine. How everything felt. It was... everything.

Like electricity sparking through every nerve ending all at once, with a heat and fluidity that made me want to rock my body.

Yes, the dark knight is good at what he does. He's damn good at making me want to cave and give in to both his desires and mine. I lick my lower lip, wincing at the cracked skin as my back stiffens and I glare at the steel door that refuses to budge.

As if knowing I was thinking about him and what he could do to me, the door to this prison opens and my hardened expression shifts to one of worry, curiosity, and eagerness.

I hadn't realized how dark it was in the room until the bright light from just beyond the cracked door makes me wince. My tired eyes sting with the need to sleep.

I suck in a small breath, but I don't cover my eyes or leave them closed for long. Pressed against the wall, I wait with bated breath until my eyes adjust.

I expect to hear the door close, but it stays open.

And the man I thought was coming in? It's not him. It's not Carter.

Thump, thump. My heart slams hard in my chest as Jase takes a step inside. Still the door stays open and my eyes have to glance at what's beyond it.

A hallway and nothing discernable, but I know it's freedom. That barely ajar door leads to freedom.

"Now don't make me regret this." The deep voice seems to echo in the small room and I swallow thickly. It's only when my throat stings and I feel as if I could choke that I realize how dry my throat is.

"Jase?" I chance a word and it makes the man smile. I remember him from the night I was taken. That's what Carter called him. He put the rag to my mouth. He's one of them.

He gives me a sexy lopsided grin that should frighten me. But instead, his charming looks put me at ease. He must be younger than Carter. His eyes are softer. But I remember them all too well, for the wrong reasons.

"You remember me?" he asks me and takes a step forward, grabbing the chair that Carter uses. He's just as tall as Carter, but leaner and in only a white t-shirt and faded jeans, he looks less threatening.

But looks are deceiving.

My lips part to speak, but I can't get out a word. A million questions are running through my head.

Why are you here? Where's Carter?

Are you going to let me go?

I can only nod.

"You're looking a little on the rough side," he says and then his voice drifts off as he looks behind him. I follow his gaze to the open door, but quickly my sights are back on his and the chair in his hand that scratches along the concrete. Turning it backward, he sits on it. As if he's deliberately acting casual.

He is. This is a setup for something. In my head, my words are strong and demanding, but when forced out they sound weak and desperate.

"What do you want?" I swallow, and this time the scratchy sensation in my throat is almost soothed. But the pain in my chest grows with every thump in my heart.

Jase breathes in deep and turns to look back over his

shoulder, toward my freedom, and then points to it with his thumb. "He doesn't seem to be taking care of you, is he?"

Thump. Another thump.

"Is this a trick?" My question is meager at best.

Jase's chuckle comes from deep in his chest and his smile widens, showing his perfect teeth.

He shakes his head. "No tricks. I just know he can be stubborn and sometimes he gets in his own way." He's being far too kind. There isn't an ounce of me that trusts him.

My gaze falls to my feet. My dirty feet and scraped knees. And then to my nails, the dirt beneath my fingers that doesn't seem to leave.

My teeth dig into my lower lip to keep me from spilling all the desperate pleas begging me to come up, but it hurts. "What does he want?"

"You." Jase's voice is soft and at ease. As if the answer was simple.

"What about me?" For the first time, my voice is as strong as I imagine it would be.

Resting an elbow on the back of the chair, Jase places his chin in his hand and considers me. He parts his lips but then closes his mouth.

"Just tell me," I beg him.

"I don't know. This..." Jase trails off, then clears his throat and looks away from me for a moment before looking me back in the eyes to continue, "isn't something he does."

"This?" I ask sarcastically, and like a madwoman, a grin forms on my face and I swear I could laugh. "Which part of this?" I dare to spit back at him. And for the first time since Jase has walked in here, pure fear pricks down my spine at the sight of his expression.

That cold, heartless look in his eyes is there and gone just as quickly as it came.

He stares ahead of him, at the cinder block wall and ignores me for a moment. I almost speak but I don't know what to say. And even if I asked the questions that keep me up at night, Jase wouldn't know the answers.

Mindlessly, I pick under my nails. Maybe if I begged him, he'd let me go. The huff of a genuine, but sarcastic laugh gets Jase's attention. I can feel his eyes on me, but I don't look up until he speaks.

"Carter said to buy you a drawing pad. But I thought maybe you'd want something else as well?"

"Sleeping pills," I answer him without thinking twice. I'm hungry, but more than that, I need to sleep. "It's hard to sleep in here."

When I peek up at him, Jase is looking at me like I'm trying to fool him and that thumping in my chest beats harder and faster. "I need to sleep," I beg him. "I take them at home. That or wine some nights. Please, I'm not trying to drug anyone or OD or anything. I just need to sleep, please." My voice cracks and that pathetic feeling that plagued me only moments before he walked through the door comes rushing back to me, hard. It nearly makes me bury my head between my knees with shame.

"I just want to sleep," I plead.

"Sleeping pills... any particular brand?" Jase's question eases the anxiety slightly.

Composing myself as best as I can, I brush my hair behind my ear and answer him, "I've tried a lot of them. There's a pink box at the drugstore. I forget the name," I say then close my eyes tight, trying to remember it. Trying to picture the box that sits on my nightstand.

They open quickly at the sound of the chair scratching on the floor.

But Jase is just leaning back, grabbing his cell phone and typing into it.

"Do you want anything else?"

"Tarot cards," I blurt out without really thinking and the expression on Jase's face tells me that I'm being stupid or naïve or weird. I don't know. I mean, even if I am losing my mind I do realize it's an odd thing to ask for. "I've been bored out of my mind and I like to think with them. It's just something I like." With each sentence, my words come out softer.

Every day I read my cards. The damn things didn't tell me this was coming though.

"Maybe clothes?" Jase asks me, giving me a pointed look and my cheeks flame with embarrassment.

"Clothes would be nice." I haven't thought much about my actual clothes; I know I'm dirty and covered in filth. The only place I've sat or slept is on this tiny mattress and I know I smell.

"I could use a lot of things-"

Jase cuts me off. "I'll get you some toiletries and you know... those things."

I nod my head, swallowing down every bit of humiliation that threatens to consume me.

"You're very nice for a prison guard," I tell him although I stare straight ahead at the empty corner of the room.

He huffs a short, humorless laugh and asks, "Food?"

"Carter said he has to be the one to feed me," I answer Jase immediately and then close my eyes as my empty stomach tightens with pain. I should have eaten before. I have to be smart. But how many times have I told myself that, only to end up in the same place with no change?

"That sounds like something he would say."

Everything hurts at this moment. My body from exhaustion, my heart from hopelessness. Starvation is only third on my list.

"What else would Carter say?" I ask him, just to continue talking. To get to know him. To make him feel like I want him to stay. My heart flickers with the hope that he may hold the key to me leaving.

"Carter would say he's sorry it had to be this way." I'd

laugh at Jase's words if they didn't hurt me the way they do.

"I don't think I believe that," I nearly whisper.

"He never wanted any of this," Jase tells me. "He was only a kid when everything escalated, and it was kill or be killed." The silence stretches as I imagine a younger version of Carter, one who hadn't been hardened by hate and death.

"You always have a choice," I manage to speak, although I find it ironic as I sit in this cell, without a single choice of my own.

"It's a nice thought, isn't it?" Jase offers. There's no sarcasm, no sense of anger or sadness. Only matter-of-fact words.

"I'd like to leave this room," I tell him although it comes out a question. As Jase nods, hope rises inside of me.

"It will happen," Jase says. "I know it will."

"Would you let me go outside at least? Or by a window for some fresh air?" Jase tilts his head and narrows his eyes as if to ask me if I think he's stupid.

"I promise I wouldn't run or anything like that. I swear." My throat tightens as he considers me.

"I'll see what I can do," is all he says to my racing heart. But it's something. It's a tiny piece of hope.

"Why are you being nice to me?" I stare into his dark eyes, willing him to answer me but inside, I hope for a lie. I want him to tell me everything is going to be okay. That he's going to get me out of here. But it's all wishful thinking.

"I'm not a nice guy, Aria, so get that out of your head." He stands abruptly and then looks back at me as he opens the door wider, so he can leave.

My blood pounds in my ears at the sight of the wide open door, with Jase's figure blocking it. His shadow fades into the darkness of the room.

Smart. I repeat it over again. Be smart.

Now is not the time. *Be his friend.* The thought hisses and I listen. He could help me. He could have mercy on me where Carter doesn't.

"I'm just following Carter's orders."

I only nod once and force myself to look elsewhere. Anywhere but toward the false sense of freedom beyond the door. He'll be back. Next time I'll be more prepared.

And with that, I'm left alone again.

CHAPTER 15

CARTER

Three hours have passed, and each hour she's more and more comfortable.

She hasn't stopped drawing since Jase left the cell. And I haven't taken my eyes off of her. There's only one camera in the room and without being able to zoom in, it's hard to see her features.

A pile of clothes and her blanket are neatly stacked and folded on the bed. But she stays on the floor, scribbling away. One page after another as if she's obsessed and unable to stop.

I need to know what she's writing down. Especially if it's some sort of account of what's happened in the last few days. A message, maybe? Maybe it has something to do with why she screams in her sleep nearly every night.

Unease creeps up my spine at the memories. I'm not surprised the first thing she asked for were sleeping pills. I can't fucking sleep anymore either. Every other night, she cries out in terror and it's only getting worse.

I thought things would change after the other day.

Another paper flies across the floor, but before its fluttering has even stopped, she's already sketching on the page that was beneath it.

Change is necessary. Even if I have to force it.

The walk from my office to the cell takes too fucking long. My fists clench tighter and my heart beats faster as I get closer.

I keep the door open and leave the chair where it is this time.

As she scoots back onto her ass and away from the piles of paper to get away from me as I approach, I lower myself to them, crouching down and picking up the closest one.

There are still a few feet between us, but the expression on Aria's face is of complete fear. Not the defiance I've grown to expect.

"Caught you off guard?" I ask her, cocking a brow. Maybe she thinks I've come to steal her gifts, or maybe the lack of food reminds her of what happened the other night. I know she ate every bit of that tray Jase gave her with her new possessions earlier today.

I wonder if she thinks it's a secret he kept from me.

"You look scared," I add when she doesn't answer my

initial question. Her doe eyes are wide, and the colors stir with so much thought and curiosity.

She doesn't answer me. She looks like she isn't even breathing as her eyes glance from the paper in my hand to the open door.

"Don't think about running, Aria. I don't want to have to take these away the second you got them."

Slowly, her chest rises and falls. Her stiff body loosens although she stays back. With her head lowered, she only peeks up at me. It's an interesting difference, the way she looks at me compared to my brother. I fucking hate it. But fear and control are everything. One day Jase will see that.

With my jaw hardened at the thought, I look down at the paper before turning it over in my hand to see what she's drawn. It's upside down at first and it takes me a moment to realize that.

It's drawn with pen, but it's beautiful. Fine little lines and sketches that depict a bleeding heart with three knives stabbed through it. The background is a storm and the ink smears only add to the emotion clearly evident on the paper. Although the knives seem to pierce through the heart easily, the rain behind it is so violent, it detracts from the knives a little.

"What is this?" I ask her without looking at her. I know she's looking at me; I can feel her careful gaze. She doesn't like to look at me when I'm looking at her. Although it's a habit I need to break, I'm more concerned with getting answers than obedience.

"The three of swords," she answers in a small voice and it beckons me to look back at her. For a moment we share a gaze, but then she drops it, focusing on the paper in my hands.

"One of your tarot cards?" I ask her and then straighten the paper in my hand, noticing how it resembles a card.

"Yes. Jase said he bought me a deck online but until they arrive I thought I would draw them myself."

I consider her for a moment. Of everything she could ask for, of everything she could be doing at this moment, this is what she chose. "Why?"

"I like to think about things and it helps me." She nervously picks at the edge of her dirty shirt where a thread has come undone. "It's been lonely, and I haven't been able to think of anything new. It was just something..." her voice trails off and she takes in a shuddering breath. Weeks of doing absolutely nothing but living with your demons would haunt and break the strongest of minds. But she's survived.

"Do your clothes not fit?"

"They do, I just get dirty doing this. So, I thought..." she pauses to take in a short breath and then another. "I just wanted to take care of this, and then I'd planned to change and try to clean myself up."

Nodding, I hand the paper back to her asking, "What does it mean?"

She's hesitant to reach out and take it, but when she does,

her fingers trace the edges of the knives. "The three of swords represents rejection, loneliness, heartbreak…" Her words aren't saddened by the information, merely matter-of-fact.

I wonder if she's lying. If the one card that she's drawn I happened to pick up, would really mean those things or if she's toying with me. She could be trying to weaken my resolve by gaining sympathy. It will never happen.

"But yours was reversed," she says, and it cuts through my thoughts of her intention.

"And what does that mean?" I ask her, expecting her to spit back that I'm the one causing it all. For her to blame all of this on me. And in so many ways it is my fault, but she's to blame as well and she doesn't even know it.

"Forgiveness," she whispers the word and then slowly inches closer to pick up each of the fallen papers, dozens of them, gathering them together and avoiding me at all costs.

The word resonates for a moment, lingering in the space between us and striking something deep inside of me.

My blood pressure rises as my eyes search her face for an indication as to what she's getting at. But she doesn't look at me and her body seems to cower more with each passing second.

The moment passes, and she neatly arranges the stack in front of her and still doesn't look up at me.

Stubborn girl. The familiar tic in my jaw begins to contract as I wait another moment. And then another before she looks up at me through her thick lashes. Instead of seeing disinterest, resentment, or whatever I was expecting, all I see is the unspoken plea for me to let her have this small bit of happiness.

But nothing in this life is free. And she should know better than that.

"When I come in here, I want you to kneel for me."

She flinches as she realizes what I've said and as her head lowers, the dip in her collarbone seems to deepen to a level that sickens me.

She's resistant to obeying, but she needs to understand. There is an expectation both of us need to meet. And what's been done can't be taken back. That's not an option. "I admire your strength. I do." I talk with her eyes on my back as I stalk to the metal chair at the far wall. I debate on leaving it there and giving her space. But that intention is quickly forgotten.

Picking up the chair, I take it back to where she's still seated, shaking her head as her shoulders hunch in.

"You keep saying I'm strong and I have to admit I don't get your humor." I'm taken aback by the severity of her tone and the venom that veils each syllable as she speaks. She offers me a smile that wavers and then adds, "Did you let him give it all to me so you could simply take it away?" Maybe the small taste of what used to be and what she could so easily have is what she needed to remember her defiance and ignite the spark between us again.

I'd love for her to fight me, but I'll only allow it after she submits.

"I'll do as I see fit," I answer simply, and she refuses to look back at me, her fingers tracing each of the papers. "All you have to do is obey me and I'll give you everything you need."

"I'd rather die." Her hazel eyes simmer with indignation as she waits for my answer. "You can have it back."

I take my time, sitting on the chair in front of her. Towering over her small frame, I lean forward and speak calmly. "My songbird, it's one thing to have the balls to say that. I respect it. But it's another to go through with it. You've already obeyed twice. And I didn't ask much, did I?"

She huffs in a tone that's both weak and strong. A manner that reflects her tortured state. So close to having what she wants and needs, and yet so close to losing everything.

"It was a cruel joke, wasn't it?" Her eyes narrow as she gazes at the door like it beckons her.

"I don't joke, Aria. Your life belongs to me. Everything you will ever get for the rest of your existence will come from me." My words come out harsh and irritated. I'm sick and fucking tired of her denying both of us. "Get. On. Your. Knees."

"Fuck you," she spits out, and instantly my fingers nearly wrap around her throat as the rough pad of my thumb rests against her lips. I can feel the rush of her blood in her neck as I grip her tightly, her gasp filling the air along with the sound of the chair scraping from the rapid movement forward.

She stiffens with my touch but she doesn't protest, staring

back at me with that burning expression as I tighten my grasp. Her breath comes out with a shudder, but she stares back at me expectantly, waiting for what I'll do next.

My heart hammers and my dick stiffens with each passing second that she holds my heated gaze. I see the moment she realizes that her hands are on my waist. Pulling herself toward me, not pushing me away.

Her eyes spark and I nearly crash my lips against hers, urging for more. Instead, I leave her there, letting a low hum of approval fall from my lips so she knows I know exactly what she's thinking.

A fire ignites between us as she grips me tighter, so tight the sound of her nails scratching against my pants is all I can hear.

"You think you shouldn't do it, simply because you've been taught it's wrong. But is that what you really want?"

"I don't want you," she says breathily, not even attempting to hide her desire.

"I won't let you ride my cock until you tell me how badly you want to cum on it." I hold her fiery gaze as I ask, "Do you understand me?"

Her body sways slightly as she holds back a strangled groan of lust.

"Humor me, Aria. I already know you're strong."

"You make me weak." Her voice breaks and the tension from the other day returns in full force. She steadies her trembling lip between her teeth.

"Is that what you're afraid of? Being weak?"

She nods her head slightly, ever so slightly. And I can see the last bit of her walls crumble for me. Crashing down to the ground in small, insignificant piles of rubble.

"I don't want you weak." I lean forward, whispering against her lips, "I want you mine."

Her eyes close and her body bends forward; she rests nearly her entire weight on me. "I will never submit to you," she says, and her words are a weak confession. As if she hates their existence.

She's close. So close. I need to offer her something.

Hope. The offer of hope is something a desperate person can never afford to pass up.

"I made a deal I shouldn't have. But I need to go through with it for as long as I have to. And it has to appear that I've done what would be expected. You're going to help me and then I'll give you whatever you want."

"What do you need me to— "

"Obey me," I say, cutting her off. "Kneel when I enter and do as I wish." My hands tingle with the sensation of feeling her so close to caving. They clench and unclench at my side.

Time passes in slow ticks as she pulls herself away from me. She can try to pretend she has somewhere else to go. But I'm her only way out of this. And eventually, she'll beg me for something. She. Will. Beg.

"Anything?" she asks, and she already knows the answer.

"Like my freedom?"

"Almost anything." I don't lie to her.

"There's nothing else--" she starts, but I cut her off. "There's always something else." My words are sharp at first but I correct myself.

"There's always something else," I repeat and then add as I stand up to leave, "It's something you so desperately need, but you don't even see it."

CHAPTER 16

ARIA

P art of what keeps me from giving in to Carter and the feelings that have been taking over my every waking moment is obvious.

The fear of the past returning. The truth in the terrors that devour my nights.

And the nightmares I remember of a past monster erase everything I've felt for Carter. There is nothing that will change that.

Sometimes it's the feeling of Stephan's hands on me that wake me up screaming. It's been so long since I've felt it. Or at least since I've been aware of it.

It used to be every single night. I couldn't sleep at all without seeing his face. Without feeling him rip me away from my mother as I begged her to stay with me. She was already gone though. Even as a child I knew she was dead.

He'd killed her.

The sleeping pills the doctor gave me at my father's request worked for a little while. Then I stopped and even though everyone else would say I was screaming, I didn't remember. I couldn't remember a single dream. Nothing but darkness as I slept.

It's come back to me though in the last few months. Even the pills can't dull the nightmares anymore. They don't stop them from lingering once my eyes have opened.

It's like I've gone back fourteen years, and my nights and days are both haunted by the memories.

"Please, Stephan," I begged him. I looked up into the eyes of the man dragging me away from her. My nails scratched and bent on the wooden floors as I kicked him, falling hard to the ground.

And he snarled, "You little bitch."

My heart races and the tears stream down my face. My fingers dig into the mattress and the sweat turns to ice along my skin. I don't know if I'm asleep or awake, but I know what's coming. I can't move; I can't breathe.

I can see myself rocking, but I'm still. I'm aware of that. It's a different time, in a different place.

I'm safe, I whisper and try to will the images away. I'm safe.

But when I open my eyes and try hard to keep from crying any more tears, I remember where I am.

It's been years since the nightmares have tortured me like this. It makes sense that they'd come back now. But without a place to hide, not in my sleep and not while I'm awake, I don't know how much longer I can go on.

I can't live like this.

I can't and I won't.

I want to call out for Carter of all things. He could hold me and take it away.

The bed beneath me groans as I roll over, and for the first time since I've been here, my back is to the door. I'm conscious of it. As conscious of it as I am the feeling of Carter's hand on my jaw. The strength, the power, the heat, and fire that lick their way up my body when he holds me like that.

Like I'm his.

I remember his words, *"I made a deal I shouldn't have. But I need to go through with it."* How he said I have to help him. I've spent weeks in this cell with no hope, until now. My imagination is wild with thoughts of what could come. But each and every one of them leads back to one scene. One that makes my thighs clench tighter.

Slowly, I lift my fingers to where his were and close my eyes as the tips of my fingers tickle my skin. The memory calms me and yet, it makes my heart beat faster.

It's his hands on me that I think of as I try to drift back to sleep. And I almost do.

But the realization of how much power he has over me with something so simple as a touch meant to control me, easing my pain steals any chance I have of falling back to sleep.

CHAPTER 17

CARTER

S*tephan.* Alexander Stephan.

It's his name screamed. He's who terrorizes her in her sleep. I know it is.

I've listened to it over and over again, each time the anger intensifying.

Last night she screamed his name.

All these nights I thought it was me causing the terrors. I thought she hated me and that she truly dreaded what I could do to her.

I've never been so fucking wrong in my life.

The door to her cell opens with a small creak, but it cries out loud in my ears as Aria's bloodshot eyes stare back at me.

"Can't sleep?" I ask her, leaving the door open and walking

with evenly paced and deliberate steps to the side of her bed.

She looks so frail beneath me. Barely eating and not sleeping for more than a few hours for over a week will take its toll on anyone. She doesn't answer me. Her eyes follow me though.

"I won't kneel," she says weakly.

"I didn't come for that."

Her brow scrunches and she nearly questions me. She knows she's disobeying, still fighting a losing battle, but my guard is down. It almost makes me smile.

"I asked for pills to sleep," she says, and her pleas are desperate. But I had to know more. There would be no pills to take it away when she wouldn't share it with me. How else would I have found out? It's her stubbornness that will make her suffer.

"I want to know how you know Alexander Stephan." Even though my words come out softly, meant to be gentle, she pales in front of me and I can see the chill spread over her body as she backs away from me.

There's only so far she can run in here and I'm tempted to grab her and force her to answer me, but I already know everything I need.

I was stupid to think I knew everything there was to know about Aria. I didn't consider anything other than who she was five years ago. I didn't consider the past that made her into that girl.

I knew her mother was murdered by a now-associate of the Romanos years before our family existed in this reality. At the time, he was the right-hand man to Talvery. Betrayal is thick in this business. Her mother's murder is what started the feud years ago, but it's been quiet for over a decade. No one's made a move since the unsuccessful retaliation on Talvery's part. Each side was simply maneuvering pieces and has been waiting for the other to strike since then.

My blunt fingernails dig into my palm as I resist touching Aria. Her back is pressed against the wall and she gathers the covers closer to her chest as if she has hope that they could save her.

But there's nothing that can save you from your past.

When she finally speaks, it's anger that threatens to come out in her voice. "Don't give me to him, please."

Anger sparks through me. This girl has a way of igniting it within me like no one else.

"You belong to me." The simple words gritted between my clenched teeth make her stiffen, but her eyes show a different response. Hope, maybe.

"Any man who thinks they can lay a hand on you will die at mine. Is that clear?"

Her eyes search mine for sincerity, even as she nods her head. "I told you, you belong to me."

The shift in her demeanor is slight. The heavier breaths, the gentle relaxation in her shoulders, and the defiance that begs to come out in the gorgeous blend of greens in her stare.

"Who is he to you?" I ask her again and watch as the cords in her slender neck tighten when she swallows.

"He killed my mother." She doesn't show much emotion; she tries to hide it, to appear devoid of it. But sadness and fear emanate from her voice.

I consider what to ask her next, but I don't want her to know what I know. If she doesn't already, she wouldn't believe me.

"Tell me more," I decide to command her, rather than asking for specifics.

She brushes the hair from her face and as she does, the blanket falls from her chest. It's only then I notice she's finally changed clothes. The thin, pale blush cotton shirt complements her complexion. Her fingers wrap around the cuffs of her sleeves as she pulls her knees to her chest.

"It's not something I like to talk about," she says simply, and then rests her cheek on her knees and looks up at me. The air is different between us. The tension of the game we've been playing isn't here and so I scoot closer to her, wondering how she'll react.

And she does. My little songbird.

She keeps the space between us, shifting to the other side of the bed and straightening her shoulders to keep her eyes on me.

The corners of my lips kick up into a half grin.

"Even now?" I ask her and the defensiveness fades, but she doesn't answer.

A moment passes, and then another. Finally, she looks toward the open door. It's the first time she's done it this morning; usually her gaze flickers to it constantly.

"You screamed his name last night," I tell her and when she looks back at me, I know she's not breathing.

"I'd like to know why," I say to finish my thought.

She swallows visibly and again pulls her knees to her chest. As she does, I inch closer. Only one. Although she stares at my hand, lying flat on the mattress and closer to her, she doesn't move away.

"I was there when he did it."

"You saw her die?"

She nods. "I was hiding. I was only playing." She shakes her head and I inch forward again, beckoning her for more. But nothing comes.

"What aren't you telling me?" My question comes out as a demand and that's when the defiance returns and the girl I'm used to seeing returns.

Her dry lips part but after several moments, she never says a word. I stand up, pushing off the thin bed and making her sway with the dip in the mattress.

"I don't like hearing you scream," I confide in her and I'm met with silence.

I turn to look over my shoulder and see her soft eyes

staring at me, brimming with unshed tears.

"I'm sorry," she apologizes to me and I find it hard to swallow as she turns her gaze from me to the blanket.

This is moving too slowly. Far too slowly. She's close to breaking and for both our sakes, I have to push her. I will not let her move backward. We're so close, and time never stops its ticking.

With that in mind, I reach down and take her blanket from her. She stares up at me like a scared child and I have to push out my words, although they come out with the control and power I always have. "You need to bathe. I don't trust you. So you'll have to trust me."

CHAPTER 18

ARIA

I've never wondered what a prisoner would feel like when led from chains to a feigned freedom. Like a courtyard or elsewhere. I wonder if they feel the same initial instinct to stay close to their warden, the way I do with Carter.

Or, maybe it's because I'm tired. I'm so fucking tired. Of fighting, of starving myself, of not sleeping. I'm not broken, but I am so fucking tired.

The rich mahogany furniture, high ceilings and carved molding accents move around me in a blur. Without shoes, my bare feet pad softly on the polished floors, and it's all I can hear.

I'm not sure if I should peek up and take in my surroundings, but every time I do, Carter gently brushes my shoulder and I instinctively pick up my pace, focused on what's to come. Still, I try to track everything, to pay attention to every doorway and window, every possible chance of escape.

My heart beats fiercely as he leads me to the right and I see a thin stream of light in the darkened hall from a room in the distance. The sounds of chatter and even laughter echo around me, although Carter pulls me in the opposite direction.

Adrenaline courses in my veins and my throat tightens.

There are other people here.

"Don't be stupid, Aria," Carter whispers in the shell of my ear, making my heart lurch and forcing me to jump back. I hadn't realized my thoughts were so obvious.

"Come," he orders me, offering me his hand. My own is small in his as he wraps his strong fingers around mine and leads me deeper down the darkened hall. All I can think about as he takes me closer to where he wants me, is that there were people here, all this time, and I have no idea if they heard my screams or what they would have done had I screamed just moments ago.

Carter unlocks a door, the clinking of metal keys accompanied by his rough voice as he says, "My brothers stay up late. They always have."

His brothers. Jase. Who else? There isn't enough curiosity in the world that could lead me to ask him. But deep in my soul, I'm crying for answers although I can already hear the hiss of the truth in the back of my skull.

There is no mercy here. Not from anyone.

The door opens with a muted creak and I only nod as he gestures for me to head inside. The small bit of hope fluttering in my chest is strangled. I can barely swallow, barely do anything but place one foot in front of the other through a large bedroom, until I hear the flick of a light switch.

The dim light flows across the black and white marble tile. Carter doesn't wait for me to enter before turning on the bath at the far side of the room. I'm struck by the sheer size of the bathroom. Even coming from wealth myself, I'm taken aback.

"It's beautiful," I speak softly. Although how I'm able to speak, I don't know.

The feel of the cold tile under my feet has never been so welcome.

The sight of the plush towel folded neatly on the counter makes me itch to touch like nothing else ever has.

The sound of a running bath has never felt so soothing. And yet, I'm so aware that I'm only a prisoner in a gilded cage, and this moment outside of the cell may be my only chance of escape.

My body is tired from not eating much and having terrors wake me every time I sleep. But I still feel the need to fight.

Carter doesn't respond to a thing I say, or to the next step I take into the bathroom, letting my fingers trail along the pale paisley pattern on the silver wallpaper. My gaze flows through the room easily but stops when I see the tub.

I can't take my eyes away from the steam that billows around the edge of the clawfoot tub.

Leaning over the spotless porcelain, Carter's back is to me with his muscular shoulders pulling his shirt tight, and I imagine how I could push him and run. I could shove him with every ounce of strength I have and run out of the room. I doubt I'd get far though, and I don't know where I'd go.

Now I know his brothers stay here. They're here somewhere.

No, I'm sure I wouldn't get far.

"I want to feed you before I bathe you." Carter's statement cuts through the visions of me running until he adds, "Strip down and get into the tub while I get your dinner."

The dead hope is resurrected; he's leaving me. The thought makes me more anxious than anything.

As he leaves, Carter grips the door and adds, "I won't be long."

Left with only the heat and comfort of the running water, my heart beats once, then twice.

My eyes close and I whisper, "Don't be stupid." The aching inside, the desperate need to run, it's all outweighed by the knowledge of what would come if I disobeyed.

Would I really deny myself a reckless chance of freedom for a warm bath? For food and his touch? Have I been so deprived that such small comforts would rate so highly?

My nails dig into my palms as I war with myself, and when my eyes open, all I see is myself in the mirror. My hair is tangled, although I've run my fingers through it daily. It's oily and dirty, which is to be expected.

My face is thin. Much thinner than I remember. Lifting the thin cotton shirt above my head, I inspect my body, running my fingers over my sides and down to my waist. The cell is so dim; I didn't see the bruises from when I was taken. The cuts around my wrists have left thin white scars, and the bruise on my ribs is an ugly shade of dark brown that's faded to nearly nothing.

I hadn't felt defeat until I was led from my cell, giving up the possibility to run only to see how damaged I've become.

The sound of the water striking against the surface harder brings my attention to the tub.

It's nearly full. The steaming hot water and relaxing fragrance of lavender bath oils Carter poured in it, beg me to cave. To let go and stop fighting. To be good and do as I'm told. If only so I can rid myself of the sense of failure and remember who I am again.

And I still remember those words he spoke days ago. He made a deal and I'm to help him. There is more to this than I know. "Be smart," I whisper to myself. I'm playing a game without knowing the rules. Without knowing the next phase. The little bit of hope and wonder push me forward toward temptation.

Turning the iron faucet, I realize it's the first thing I've touched in weeks beyond the few items in the cell. Something as simple as turning a knob feels both foreign and nostalgic. I never want to go back to the cell. My chest feels hollow as I think, *never*, but I know that the choice isn't mine.

It is, a small voice murmurs in the back of my head. The voice that takes advantage of my pain and promises so much hope in whispers of deceit.

Jasmine and lavender fill my lungs as I inhale the calming scents and quickly remove my shirt and shove my cotton pants down my legs. Although the clothes are new, they're still dirty. Everything in that cell is dirty.

The fabric clings to my toes and I have to kick it off and toward the puddle of clothes. Just as I do, I hear the heavy footsteps of Carter coming back.

Fear keeps me from moving for only a moment, but then I quickly place a foot into the steaming water, hissing at the onslaught of heat and causing the water to splash around the tub. Water hits the floor as I move to step with my other foot into the hot bath, the heat becoming more and more welcoming as my body adjusts to it. With my back to the door, I hear Carter enter, but I ignore him, lowering myself into the tub filled with a warmth I so desperately needed. And hide myself from him.

"How does it feel?" Carter's voice carries through the

room with a powerful resonance.

Like heaven, I think as I turn slowly, careful not to splash the water, but also careful to stay under and somewhat hidden beyond the white bubbles on the surface.

I try to tell him that it feels wonderful and thank him when I finally meet his gaze, but I'm silenced by the intensity within. His eyes swirl with the danger of a man close to getting what he wants. An animalistic heat passes between us and I can only nod for fear of what my voice would sound like if I dared utter a word to him.

Thankfully, he tears his gaze from me and picks up a ceramic plate from the counter.

"You need to eat." Carter's command sounds more like a reminder to himself. And again, I merely nod.

I've had delicious food before. I've gorged myself on delicacies without thinking twice. It's one of the only benefits of my upbringing. But the food Carter brought me makes my mouth water and my grip tighten on the tub to keep me from ripping the plate from his hands.

He must see my eagerness; he always smiles that devilish grin when he knows I'm eager. Bastard.

"Open," he commands me and like a good girl, my lips part and I nearly moan when he slips me the small chunk of filet dipped in au jus with a dab of herbed butter smeared across the top. The meat melts in my mouth, the tastes singing on my lips. My eyes are still closed as I relish the food, thinking it's the most delicious thing I've ever eaten when Carter brushes another piece against my lips.

Instantly I open my lips for him, and his finger brushes against my tongue as he gives me a second piece and then another. My teeth scrape against his fingers and my eyes widen with worry that he thinks I did it on purpose, but he only feeds me more.

The fear and worry slip away, just as the time does with each slice of tender meat.

Blistered tomatoes and peppers along with roasted potatoes find themselves in the mix as Carter feeds me until my stomach is full and I can't take another bite. It's been so long since I haven't felt hunger pains. It feels like forever since I've sunk into a deep tub, covered in hot water. I rest my head against the side of the tub and pretend like everything is alright. It's only a small moment until the clinking of the ceramic plate on the tile floor disturbs me and brings me back to the present.

My body stiffens slightly, sloshing the water toward the edge of the tub away from Carter as he dips a washcloth into the tub.

His fingers brush against my skin and sinfully, I welcome the touch. It's been so long, and I've been so lonely. I want more. I need more. I find myself wishing for him to take me like I know he wants to.

Has he really broken me so easily? Or is this something I

should want the way I do? The questions bring a haze to my mind and a thrumming in my blood. The washcloth travels over my body, starting at my feet and working its way upward. My calves, my thighs and so close to between them.

I know he can hear my heavy breathing; he can see how I grip the edge of the tub. But he doesn't touch me there. Instead, he tells me to wet my hair and takes his time massaging my scalp and lathering my hair. The scent of the chamomile shampoo overwhelms me, and I hum ever so slightly until I hear it and stop myself.

Everything feels so good.

"Back under, songbird," he tells me in that velvety voice. The voice I don't want to disobey, and so I don't. I do as he says. With every command he gives me, I do exactly what he says.

He massages the washcloth over my shoulders and I whimper as he kneads the pain away. I hadn't realized how much my body ached until he showed me so. A low groan of approval forces me to open my eyes and stare into his. But he's not looking at my gaze. His eyes are focused on my hardened nipples, peeking up from the water.

The washcloth makes a splash as it hits the water and slowly sinks to the depths of the tub. Carter lets his fingers trail down my chest, plucking one of my nipples and then the other. It happens slowly, his fingers determined but also giving me a warning. His rough thumb circles them first before tugging on them and causing my head to fall back and my thighs to clench. Each tweak sends a sharp spike of need between my legs, and I nearly spread them for him. My clit pulses with need. I feel it so strongly I don't think it would take much at all for me to cum for him. And I can't find it in me at all to find any shame at that fact.

The dull desire that hasn't faded, shoots through me and I welcome it.

Carter's dark eyes find mine, but instead of reaching lower, his arm dips into the water next to me and he gathers the washcloth once again.

I'm reminded of his patience. How slowly he does everything. I don't know if he finds pleasure in teasing me or if it's simply that he doesn't want this moment to end, but either way, I lean my head back as he continues bathing me, and I don't object until his hand is right where I've secretly been wishing for it to be.

He brushes the washcloth against my throbbing clit and I gasp, moving away from the intense pleasure and making waves in the tub that splash over the edge. Fear and desire mix into a confusing potion that I drank long ago. And at this moment, I'd drink the bottle again, I'd suck it dry and lick the edge of the neck where the last beads of liquid would gather. That's how badly I wish for him to do it again.

"Don't let go, Aria. If you do, I'll stop," he warns me and my lungs still. My body's on fire with need. I slowly lower myself back under the warm water, until my breasts are hidden again, and I hold Carter's eyes as I slowly reach back up and grip on to the edge. My body's still, so still as Carter's gaze flickers between my pussy and my stare. I bite down on my bottom lip as he reaches between my legs again.

His movements have been steady and slow. Careful and considerate even. But as the washcloth falls into the water, brushing against my thigh and ass, and his fingers replace the cloth, his movements are nothing but savage.

He shoves his fingers inside of me. My back bows as the sudden spike in pleasure crashes through every inch of my body.

"Carter," I whimper his name as he pushes his palm against my clit. I've never been touched like this. Air is torn from me and I can't breathe or move or do anything but grip tighter and try to stay still as he finger fucks me harder and harder.

"Carter," I cry out his name louder into the hot air and grip the edge of the tub as hard as I can. I can't let go but my body is begging for me to run, to move, to both get closer to the intense pleasure and to leave it quickly.

I know when I do cum, it will split me into pieces and he'll love how I shatter under his touch. It both terrifies me and thrills me.

I should be ashamed as I writhe in the water. I should be embarrassed as he hisses when my pussy clamps around his fingers and my orgasm tears through me, coming faster and harder than it ever has before.

My heart shouldn't pound for more. My body shouldn't ache for more. I shouldn't sit up so quickly with the intention of gripping his wrist and pleading with him for more. The waves are still crashing through me as he turns around, grabbing the towel and ignoring how I've just come apart for him.

My fears cloud the desire; they dim the sensation of lust that ricochets through my blood, my breathing steadying.

But when he turns to face me, I know it's alright. I know I did well to let him touch me. From the way he looks at me, it's like he's never wanted anything more in his life.

CHAPTER 19

CARTER

She's too good. Too fucking perfect.

And that's how I'll keep her so that each and every time I can ruin her. It's a delicate balance, knowing what to offer her and when to take from her.

Tonight, I've given more than enough, and I'll feel her break beneath me. I'll feel her shatter under me as I take every bit of her that I want. And she'll fucking love me for it.

The water falls around her in a patter onto the tile floor. She lets it drip down her back and sides. Even the thick towel I'm wrapping around her waist can't hide her from me. I've felt every inch. Every curve is burned into my memory.

Her skin trembles beneath my fingertips as I brush them against her shoulders.

I take my time, letting each small touch catch her off guard. The gasps and sharp breaths only add to the thrill. My cock is harder than it's ever been as I lead her to the bedroom and she clings to that towel as if she'll be able to keep it.

Her small frame casts a shadow on the thick carpet, the moonlight shining through the drapes. I can practically hear her heart beating as she stares at the bed. My fingers slip over her silky skin and I let my lips fall to her shoulder, so I can whisper, "You don't need this anymore." My fingers slip between the plush towel and her soft skin. I half expect my songbird to object. To continue to pretend like she doesn't want this.

But to my surprise and delight, she lets the towel fall and gently steadies her back against my chest when I take that small step forward, discarding the distance between us.

My fingers dip into her cunt, her hair tickling my fingers as I pet her still-swollen clit. I'm rewarded with her ass pushing against my cock, her back bowing, and a small moan that's barely muffled.

"It's my turn, Aria," I say, and my voice nearly trembles at her name when I feel her thighs tighten around my fingers. "Are you ready again so soon?" I turn her around, her small breasts a beautiful flushed color and her bottom lip drops in surprise like she's been caught.

"You're eager to cum again and feel that sweet, sinful torture paralyze your body?" I take a half step forward, forcing her ass to bump against the bed.

"I bet I could make you cum just from sucking these," I tell her and pull her pale petal pink nipples between my middle and pointer fingers. I tug on both at once. Her head lolls slightly, but those beautiful hazel eyes stay on mine as she moans.

"Sit." I give her a simple command. And she obeys. I can't describe the pride, the satisfaction from watching her so eagerly waiting for another command. "Good girl," I add, the words slipping out easily, and my hand rests gently on her thigh. I move it upward until I grip her ass and toss her higher onto the bed.

"Show me your cunt." Her cheeks blaze a bright red, even in the darkness, but letting her head fall back and staring at the ceiling, she parts her legs and then bends her knees, digging her heels into the comforter beneath her so I can see my prize.

"Look at me," I tell her, surprised by my own irritation. Her eyes instantly find mine, widened slightly. "Watch me. I want you to know how I look at you. What I think of you. Do you understand me?" She doesn't hesitate to nod. And glancing between her face and her spread pussy lips, I make sure she's watching me intently.

My fingers trace along her lips, soft and wet with arousal. Goosebumps travel over her thighs and she shivers when I gently push on her swollen nub. Her back arches off the bed as my fingers slip over her entrance and then back up.

"Beautiful," I say the one word, and that gorgeous blush in her chest creeps to her cheeks. I'm careless as I rip my shirt off on my way to the nightstand.

I have two sets of cuffs, but I'll only use one pair tonight. Pulling the door open, I grab the set and grip her wrist to move it where I want it. Her inhalation of surprise is met with the sound of the cuffs tightening, one on her wrist and one on the bedpost. Outstretched, she struggles not to object.

I can tell by the way she readjusts herself that she knows what's coming. I unbuckle my pants and she stills; they fall to the floor and my stiff cock juts out. I've never known how badly my cock could ache to be inside of a woman. Until now.

Gripping it and stroking once, precum already beads at the head.

My gorgeous Aria whimpers with need.

"Spread your legs for me." Before I'm finished speaking the words, she's already obeyed.

"I've waited so long for this," I admit to her as I crawl up the bed and over her small frame. My hips fit between her thighs and my cock nestles in her pussy as I lower my lips to the crook of her neck.

I've agonized over how I'd fuck her the first time. Whether I'd make her ride me so she couldn't deny how badly she wanted me. I wasn't sure if I'd be slow and steady, making her scream for me to fuck her harder as she got closer to the edge of her orgasm.

But now that the time has come, I realize how selfish I am. How truly and deeply to the core selfish I am.

All I want to do is take what's mine. To slam myself inside her to the hilt and fuck her like she's my whore. Mine and mine alone.

And that's exactly what I do. In one swift stroke, I ravage her. Her tight pussy is already hot and wet and eager for my cock. She takes all of me and screams out a sweet sound of utter rapture. With her free hand, her nails rake down my chest as her heel digs into my ass.

The need to keep still inside of her while she cums violently on my cock is overridden by the desire to piston my hips and rut between her legs. The sweet smell of her arousal and the sounds of our flesh smacking together repeatedly are everything I'll need to justify what I've done.

She struggles under me, her shoulders digging into the mattress with each hard thrust. Every time I pound into her, she responds like she was made just for me. The tightening of her pussy, the strangled cries, and sweet tortured moans are better than I ever could have imagined.

Her nails dig into my shoulder as I keep a relentless pace. My balls draw up and my spine tingles with the desire to cum deep inside of her.

But I need more. Gritting my teeth, I fuck her harder and faster until a cold sweat breaks out on my skin.

She screams out again, but the scream is different this time.

It's pain. It's reflected in her face too. My heart sinks in my chest until I see her wrist, being pulled against the metal cuff.

Fucking hell. I'm agitated and reckless as I climb over her, her arousal covering my dick as I dig in the nightstand for the key to unlock the fucking cuff.

It takes longer than I'd like and when it's finally free, I don't waste a second to grip her hips, then flip her over so she's on her knees with her ass in the air. She yells out in surprise, but it's silenced when I slam all of me back into her welcoming heat.

The sweet sounds filling the air are heaven. With every thrust, she cries out in pleasure.

I grip her ass with both of my hands, nearly cumming with her as she spasms on my cock. Her nails dig into the sheets and her thighs tremble with the ripple of her release.

I wanted her to beg for it. In the tub, in my bed. I wasn't going to let her cum until she was begging for me to fuck her.

But the best-laid plans never do work out.

And as I thrust into her with an unrelenting pace, feeling her struggle to stay on her knees until she finally falls beneath me while I rut into her savagely and she screams out incoherently with pleasure, I realize I'd rather have her beg me to stop. I'd rather take every ounce of pleasure from her until she can't take any more.

Until she's limp and spent and can do nothing but hold on to the comforter beneath her as if it can save her from me.

CHAPTER 20

ARIA

I've never felt so deliciously used and bared by someone so savagely.

My body aches as it has for weeks, but in a different way. In a way that makes me feel like my body will give in and collapse if I try to move. As I roll over in the bed, I can still feel him inside of me. Taking everything and pushing me over the edge, time and time again. The reminder sends a wanting desire through my blood.

He fucked me like he owned me.

Because he did.

He does still.

The thought makes my eyes pop wide open. My gaze travels slowly over the brightly lit room with gray walls and a tray ceiling painted even darker. The room has a sense of power to it. It's bold and dangerous even. Sharp and modern furniture and not a thing out of place.

Except for me.

My body is still, knowing I'm in Carter's room.

Not in the cell; a breath leaves me slowly, as quietly as I can allow it. I never want to go back there.

I don't hear anything. Not a sound. Another moment passes, and slowly I will myself to reach behind me, searching for Carter's presence, any sign that he's sleeping next to me.

I find nothing but the chill of empty sheets.

It takes me longer than I'd like to admit to have the strength and will to turn over, still pretending that I'm sleeping. But after moments of sensing no one else in the room, I take a chance to look around and find the room empty and the bedroom door open.

I take in his bedroom as slowly as I did the other side and wait for a sign that Carter's here. But there's no trace of him.

A pile of vibrant clothes, at odds with the bright white comforter, catches my attention.

Daring to sit up and wincing from the dull ache between my legs, I cautiously pick them up and find a silk robe and negligee that I would never wear.

It's scandalous and for the body of a model. It makes no sense that my initial thought is that he's going to be disappointed with me. That I could never do this delicate combination of lace and silk justice. Other than to justify it with the thought that if I disappoint him, he'll send me back. And I never want to go in that cell again. Never.

I don't even realize I'm clutching the fabric to my chest until Carter's voice pierces through the threatening thoughts.

"What's wrong?" he asks as he enters the room.

My head shakes of its own accord, making my hair tickle my bare shoulders as I do and reminding me that I'm naked.

I should have searched through his things. I should have tried to escape. A bulleted list of all the ways I've disappointed myself weighs heavily on my chest as I watch him pull one drawer open and then the next until he sets a pair of metal handcuffs down on the dresser.

His casual stance is a façade; power still radiates around him. Carter stalks toward me.

I'm only moving from the cell where I could deny him, to his bed where I'll be his whore.

"If you don't like it, there are more." Carter's tone is dismissive at best and I don't know what he's referring to until he nods at the ball of clothes in my hand.

I let the fine fabrics fall onto the comforter, not knowing how to answer. I'm on pins and needles as I sit here trying to decide what I need to do to keep myself safe and in the best possible position to gain my freedom back.

"I like you nervous." Carter's voice draws my eyes back to him. He looks more casual today than I've ever seen him.

It's not the clothes he wears, but his posture and the way he stalks toward me. Stopping at the edge of the bed, I get a strong whiff of his scent and I hate how much I love it. Even more so I hate how my thighs clench and the twinkle of a grin threatens to pull at his lips when I whimper.

"I enjoyed you last night," Carter's voice rumbles in a way that ignites my nerve endings on fire. Reaching out to cup my chin in his hand, he stares at my lips, running his thumb along the bottom one.

And something shifts inside of me. This is a man with so much power and control, someone who could destroy me and in many ways has already. Yet all I want in this moment is for him to kiss me. He hasn't yet, and deep inside a part of me needs it.

But his thumb stops the soothing motions and his expression falls as he speaks, although it's worded as a question. "You haven't eaten?"

"I only just woke up." The words come out like an excuse with a plea coating them. The weak sound on my lips disgusts me. I was stronger in the cell. I breathe in harsher, knowing I'd bite back a quip if only my ass was on the thin mattress in the dark cell in this moment.

But I don't want to go back. I'm ashamed to know it so clearly and to hold onto that truth like I'll die if it slips from me. In an effort to diminish my hate of that pathetic fact, I remind myself that are far more chances of escape out here.

And there is nothing but agony in that cell. The ache of loneliness and starvation and sleepless nights filled with past pains.

I refuse to go back.

Carter's touch falls as he turns away from me, back to the dresser. "There's breakfast in the kitchen. If you see anyone, ignore them and they'll ignore you. Understood?" He tosses the cuffs inside a drawer and searches for something else.

I nod once when he glances over his shoulder, although inside I'm reeling. All I can think is that there may be someone here to save me. Someone to show mercy. Maybe Jase? Or else I can run.

"Verbal responses, little songbird," he says casually as if he's telling me what the weather is. The drawer shuts tight with finality and I find myself nodding my head again as I answer him, "Yes," with my eyes fixated on the metal peeking through his clenched hand.

"And you'll wear this," he tells me as he holds up a thin chain. Every inch or so there's a small pearl, alternated with diamonds. It's long, so long it would fall to nearly my belly button and as I take it in I see the diamonds grow larger as you near the end. There, in the center, is a large tear-shaped diamond.

But all that sparkles is only sin disguised in beauty.

"A collar?" My heart beats like a war drum inside my chest. He must hear the defeat on my tongue.

"You can't collar a songbird, Aria, but you can tether one or cage it. The choice is yours."

"Either the cell or the necklace?" I ask him to clarify, and just the idea that I can save myself from going back there has my hand reaching for the necklace.

Carter nods once, and my eyes are brought back to his.

"Turn around," he orders me, the fire flickering in his eyes. Steadying my breathing, I turn my back to him and feel the sweet sensation of a shiver run down both my front and back as he moves my hair to the side. My nipples harden as the cool diamonds and pearls fall down my chest and over the crook of my shoulders and neck. Carter lets his hands trail to my breasts once he's done, his hot breath tickling the shell of my ear as he whispers, "Beautiful."

But just as quickly as he's shown me gentleness, he leaves me, his absence intensifying the coldness of the air. And I'm left naked on my knees in his bed. Wearing a collar and making decisions based on fear.

Thoughts of my father and Nikolai return. Shame accompanies the image of their disapproval and disgust. As much as I'd like to lie, I loved what Carter did to me last night and I'd let him do it again.

"Why are you doing this to me?" The words are torn from the other side of me. The side I want to hide and tell to be quiet.

Walking back to the dresser, I think Carter's ignored me until he answers, "Because I can," he answers in a tone not to be questioned or defied. "A man asked me what I wanted, and I could buy anything I want, yet I saw your picture and knew I could never have you." He turns to face me, leaning against the dresser and waiting for my response.

I remember the words I've held so dearly that he spoke days ago. The words that gave me hope. How I would help him and he would give me everything. I wonder if it's a lie, or if what he's telling me now has anything to do with that deal he shouldn't have made.

"And now that you've..." I trail off, then swallow my words.

"I don't have you, Aria. Not yet. But when I do, you'll be begging me to stay." What strikes the most fear in my heart is how utterly and completely I believe him.

Walking toward me, I can see something begging to escape from his lips. Something that's maybe a secret, maybe not. But he merely runs his fingers along my lips again and tells me he'll find me when he's ready for me again before leaving me and keeping the bedroom door open.

When something is hard to the touch and so sharp it would draw blood, you have to always be careful. It's the gentleness of it that will break you. You can't ever let your guard down.

If you're smart, you avoid it and if you have to be around it, you stay away from the parts that hurt. But those aren't the parts that destroy. It's the parts that you begin to crave, the parts you don't want to resist that bring you to your knees.

They make you forget or maybe they make you think the sharpness won't cut you, as if you're somehow immune or no longer prey to it.

Even knowing so, I fall helpless to the way he cups my chin like that. And I sit there for far too long with my fingertips lingering where I can still feel him.

I can't breathe as I wake up. The cold sweat that covers my skin makes me shake, as does my racing heart. The room is dark, and I can't see for a moment, but the hands gripping my shoulders and holding me down aren't the ones in my nightmare.

It's not Stephan, I try to think logically as I hear Carter's voice yelling at me to wake up.

My chest heaves as the light filters into my vision and I see him. The anger in his tone is absent from his pained expression.

My shoulders hunch forward as I try to calm down. It was just a night terror. I can't control them. I can't stop them.

"Please don't send me back," I barely push out and it causes Carter's fingers to dig deeper into my shoulders before he releases me. Stalking to a chair on the far side of the bedroom, he sits with his body leaning forward, his dark eyes staring at me through the dark room.

My skin tingles with a numbing fear. I can't go back to the cell. Tears leak from my eyes at the thought that one fear of mine, a man who destroyed my world and threatened to do more, would keep me from being safe from yet another, the cell.

"Please," I plead weakly and before the word is completely spoken, Carter commands me, "Come here."

Although my body feels weak, I force my limbs to move quickly as they fight with his sheets. I practically fall to the ground and quickly crawl to him, the rug brushing against my knees.

In nothing but a pair of silk pajama pants, his abs ripple in the faint moonlight. His body looks like it was carved in marble. Even with the fear still strongly present, I can feel the itch of my fingers to run down the carved lines of his muscles. If nothing else, he's a beautiful distraction. He can use me, fuck me into a deep sleep. And I would beg for it in this moment.

I'd beg him to use me and take away everything else.

I slow my pace as I get closer to him, the necklace nearly dragging on the ground. Its presence makes my nakedness very much at the forefront of my mind. His knees are parted, and I settle in between them. In the darkness and with that look in his eye, he radiates power as I kneel at his feet.

Slowly, I reach my hands up to his thighs in the silence. He hasn't said a word, but I'm sure I have to please him. I can't go back to the cell. Not over this.

My fingers slip between the silk fabric and his hot skin at the deep V on his hips.

My actions are cut short and my heart lurches when Carter's strong fingers grab my wrist and yank my hand away. I can barely breathe as the intensity in his gaze ignites.

The silence stretches as he stares at me and I feel helpless, not knowing what he wants.

"Get on all fours," he commands me, barely loosening his grip so I can quickly obey him. My heart thumps so hard it's all I can hear.

"Face on the floor," he tells me, and I do as he says, keeping my ass in the air. "Palms up and at your knees," Carter tells me and again I do as he says, but he repositions them. All the weight of my body is on my shoulders and neck as I lay my head on the floor and my arms stay behind me, not useful in balancing or aiding me in any way. I'm completely bared to him and at his mercy.

A moment passes and then another as Carter paces around me. I try to swallow, but I can't. The fear of him finding me less than pleasing makes my knees tremble, and he only responds by moving my legs farther apart. The moment I close my eyes, his deep and rough voice commands me to open them and look at him. Towering over me, I have no idea what my dark knight thinks of me or what he plans to do to me.

"Tell me what you were dreaming of," he finally says, and I answer him, the rug rubbing against my cheek and my breath feels hot against my face.

"I don't remember," I tell him and although it's true, I know what the terrors consist of.

"It wasn't important to you? Not important enough to remember?" he asks as he crouches behind me. I can't see him, but I can feel him. I can always feel Carter's unyielding presence.

"No," I shake my head against the ground and answer him how I think he wants me to. "It's not important and I'm sorry," I tell him, and the silence stretches.

My body jolts forward as his hand brushes against my ass. The rough pad of his thumb follows down to my pussy, gently trailing along my clit and then back up. He grips my ass cheek in a bruising manner and my eyes shut tight as I prepare for more.

Whack! His hand slaps against my ass and forces a cry from my lips. I sink my teeth into my lip and take another. The sharp stinging pain is accompanied by his hand sliding up my front, so he can roll my left nipple between his fingers. The combination of pain and pleasure is directly linked to my clit. My body rocks to the side, unable to stay still as he pulls my now hardened peak.

He instantly releases me to push down on my upper back between my shoulder blades, and he spanks the same spot on my ass again. Biting down on my lip, changes the cry to a muffled whimper and the pain that shoots up my body ignites every nerve ending in my body, heating my core and stealing my breath.

Panting against the rug, I wait for more. I can feel my pussy clench around nothing, praying for pleasure to take the pain away. His splayed hand on my back travels along my spine, leaving a trail of goosebumps. I can feel his breath against my ass before he bites down, making my mouth form an O with both surprise and something else. The pain is nothing like what I expect and my body trembles with delight at the thought of more.

Quickly, he pulls away and another sharp smack meets my heated skin, this one sending tears to my eyes. The pain and intensity have gathered into a ball in the pit of my stomach and I don't know that I can take anymore.

"Please," I whisper, but I don't know what I'm asking for.

"Why am I punishing you, Aria?" His deep voice is a soothing balm to my broken cries.

"Because I woke you," I answer him as I feel his hips brush against the backs of my thighs. He settles behind me and lowers his lips to my shoulder. He plants a small kiss on my shoulder as the head of his cock gently presses into my entrance. It's only a tease and I find myself rocking backward, praying he'll fuck me and take the pain away.

His hot breath tickles the crook of my neck as he whispers, "Because you lied to me."

I can't respond because he immediately slams inside of me and fucks me exactly how I wanted him to.

CHAPTER 21

CARTER

"There are five wings in the estate. And each has their own lock." I glance down at Aria, listening to her bare feet pad on the marble tile as we enter the foyer. The double-doored entrance is only feet away and I know she's resisting the urge to look at it.

"There are locks everywhere, inside and out." She chances a peek at me and stills when she meets my gaze. "I often invite those who I don't consider friends here and sometimes I don't want them to leave."

She's silent as she considers what I've said. Nervousness trickles down her body. It's in the way she swallows, the way she holds her hands in front of her. The way she almost trips over her own feet. And I love her nervousness.

"The front door, for instance." I motion toward it and she turns stiffly as if she wasn't dying to look at it. "That box there, to the right of it. You need a code to open it, from either inside or out."

"I thought you said it was one or the other." Her soft voice is questioning. Her hazel eyes peer up at me as if I've wronged her. As if I've hurt her. "You said a bird can be tethered or caged, not both."

A smile tickles my lips as I reply, "Haven't you learned that all you need to do is ask?"

Her lips turn down into a frown, but she stays quiet. She knows she's caged. Wherever she goes, she will go with me, caged and protected just the same.

"I'm a prisoner," she says as her voice cracks, and she looks longingly at the front doors. The architecture foreboding in a way that seems to forbid a guest from leaving.

"You were before in your father's home." My voice is deep and echoes in the foyer. Her eyes reach up to mine in shock as I continue, "Afraid to leave. Afraid to do anything without permission."

"I wasn't afraid," she whispers, and I know she's well aware of the lie she's spoken.

"You let fear rule you. Don't lie to me." Unease trickles through me. The realization of what she truly fears could change everything.

"How do you know what I did and didn't do?" she asks

weakly, denying the truth and deflecting her attention to something else.

Since she lied to me, I present a lie to her in return. "When you were offered to me, I did my research. I have friends in your father's army of men. Eyes and ears who offer information for a certain price. I know you spent almost all of your time alone in your room. Maybe that's why it took so long for you to obey me. You're used to cells."

Her mouth parts, no doubt with a rebuttal, but wisely she slams it shut before a word is spoken.

Time passes as we move on. Both of us quiet. Both of us in our own world of denial.

"Your things can be moved to my office, den, or the bedroom. The drawing pad and whatever else you want," I offer her but still, she's quiet. Her fingers fidget with one another throughout the tour of the two wings she's allowed to enter. She doesn't seem to look at anything or notice anything at all unless we pass a window, which, as I pointed out, have locks on them as well.

"Why are there five wings?" she asks me as I lead her to the grand kitchen. She still hasn't eaten and she needs to. There's no reason for her not to and the threat of sending her back to the cell if she doesn't, is so close to being spoken to life. I'd rather save it for something else, something more meaningful. But my little bird needs to eat.

"I had four brothers and decided they should each have

their own wing," I tell her and step into the kitchen. The garden is just beyond the back wall, lined with black glass from floor to ceiling. The floors are a dark walnut and polished so smoothly I can see our reflection in them.

Her eyes move across the sleek, modern kitchen, from the high-end cabinets to the white granite countertops. Everything is done in white. It's clean and modern and balances the black glass perfectly.

I anticipate her saying many things, but not the next words that spill from her lips.

"I'm sorry."

My forehead pinches with a deep crease. "For what?" I question.

"You said you had four brothers. I take it that one or more have passed?" She turns to face me and her hip brushes one of the stools to the island. I can tell she's not sure if she should sit or not, and I leave her wondering. Just like I leave the pangs of regret and sadness to settle in my gut. Instead, I focus on how discerning Aria is. She's a deadly combination of beautiful and perceptive. I need to remember that.

"Carter," Jase calls out from behind me and when I turn his steps slow. His eyes drift from where I am, almost blocking Aria from view, and then to her.

"I didn't realize you were busy," he says to me although his eyes travel down Aria's body. Even with her robe tied tightly with the sash and covering her décolletage, she looks like she was made to tempt.

"What is it?" I ask him and again he looks at her. From my periphery, I watch her glance at the floor and those fingers of hers continue making tight knots around one another.

Gripping the back of her neck, just slightly, she stops her fidgeting.

They both want to know what she is to me. I can see it written on their faces as much as I can feel the tension in the air.

It doesn't matter what she is, so long as they all know she's mine.

Even more, I know Jase is questioning the way I hold her at this moment and why she's out of the cell. Maybe he's wondering how long I'll keep her out here. Or how long I'll keep her period.

I make soothing strokes with my thumb along the back of her neck as Jase tells me something about a car. I don't know what the fuck he's talking about. I don't give a damn either. I assume it's some update about the supply, but he doesn't want to speak openly in front of Aria.

My little songbird relaxes under my touch, peeking up at me every so often. I know she's wondering what he thinks of her.

"Aria," I say her name in the middle of whatever Jase was saying and he falls silent. "I'd like you to step outside, so I can talk to Jase." All I can hear is her breathing in this moment. The fear, the hope, the surprise of her surroundings. My poor Aria knows so little. But she'll learn.

She quickly nods but she doesn't move until my hand slips down her back, leaving a trail along the silk. Jase stays by the island, his hands in his pockets as I lead her to the door. It's black glass as well and blends into the wall, only opening when a verified print is pressed against the biometric security panel. Aria watches intently, but she wouldn't be able to open it if she tried and with fifteen-foot walls around the garden and a guarded fence around the estate, she won't be able to run.

I can see it on her face when the realization registers with her.

"And when I'm done with this conversation, it's back to the bedroom." I lean in closer to her and whisper in her ear, "I'm going to fuck you until I've had my fill."

The sound of Jase's footsteps lets me know he's coming as I watch Aria walk into the garden, letting the sun hit her face as if it's the first time she's ever experienced it.

"I have Jared on the lookout at the club. We'll have a list of the heavy buyers of S2L by the end of the week."

"Perfect," I answer him although I watch Aria walking deeper into the garden to lie on a patch of grass. "Anything else?"

"Talvery knows we have her."

A smile pulls my lips up. "It took him long enough. One of Romano's men leaked it?"

I turn to Jase, who's watching Aria as he nods. "It couldn't stay secret forever." He turns to look at me before adding,

"He'll come for her."

"He'll want to," I correct him. "But which of his men would be willing to come here and die for her?"

"She speaks highly of Nikolai," Jase offers, and I can see the hint of a smile on his face. Aria's first week in the cell gave me plenty of information as she talked out loud to nothing but brick walls, begging for help and companionship. Nikolai's name slipped from her lips nearly every single fucking day.

"Let him come. He can be the first of them to die."

CHAPTER 22

ARIA

The smell of coffee is what wakes me, and without thinking I roll over in the large bed, stretching before I'm even fully awake. The soothing ache of my muscles is comforting, as is the gentle fragrance of clean linens and the hint of a masculine scent that makes my core both ache and heat.

And then I remember.

It's always like this.

I've been out of the cell for three days, and yet when I wake up in Carter's bed, it takes me a moment to remember. Maybe I don't want to admit that it's real. Maybe a part of my subconscious is far away from here. But each morning I have to remember.

Slowly, I calm my beating heart and wait for a noise, any

sign that he's here. He's a sinful addiction, creeping into my blood and fueling the lust and fire for the forbidden. I crave him, his acceptance, his dominance, and yet I'm so aware that's all wrong. That small voice that whispers there must be a way out of here is getting quieter by the day. That's what scares me the most.

Three mornings I've woken up in Carter's bed, and just like the last two, he's not here.

Not physically, but he's watching. I learned the hard way yesterday, only the second day of being out of the cell. I thought I couldn't waste another day, listening and obeying. I had to try to find a way out of here. The memory forces my gaze to the dresser.

I was snooping. How could I not? He wasn't here, and I still have no way out of his grasp. No one comes in and no one goes out. The place is a fortress and I its prisoner.

And so, drawer after drawer, I slipped them open, hoping to find something. I'm not sure what. A gun or a weapon.

I'm not sure he'd listen to me if I made demands and held him at gunpoint, or that I'd be successful in rushing him or forcing him to let me go. Somehow, I find it hard to believe, but still, I had to try.

My eyes close and my body tenses, remembering his deep voice and how it shook me to the core. The drawer slammed shut as I screamed out and dared to look over my shoulder at Carter leaning against the doorframe.

"Kneel." The one word I've refused over and over from Carter brought me to my knees. My words tripped over one another as I tried to apologize or hide what I was doing.

But I've always been a terrible liar and he knew better.

"Open your mouth." Hearing him give me the command made my pussy hot and clench with desire. He throat fucked me. A punishment, I suppose, but it's not what it was for me.

With my fingers digging into my thighs, my eyes burning, and my breath cut from me, he shoved himself down my throat. And I was nothing but wet for him.

The fear was still present. It's always present. The knowledge that when he was done using me, he could send me back to the cell kept that fear very much alive.

He wasn't done with me when he pulled away and allowed me to breathe again. As I heaved for air, he forced me to all fours. Shamefully, my face turned hot as it hit the rug and he slammed inside of me. My back tried to arch as I moaned a ragged, strangled sound of pleasure.

I came nearly instantly, and Carter stilled deep inside of me. Gripping the hair at the base of my skull, he forced me to arch my back and whispered in my ear, "You fucking love what I do to you." And I couldn't deny it.

I fucking loved it. But it was a punishment and I was reminded of that and what I'd done before he left me panting and sated on the floor.

"Next time it will be the cell." His words ring clear in my

head as I glance at all the drawers I have yet to open.

I may love the way he fucks me, but that doesn't change much. I don't fight the urges anymore. I want them, and they help me to survive, but it doesn't make me any less ashamed, because I know very well I'm a prisoner here and Carter can do with me as he wishes.

Although I crave my freedom, that doesn't mean I don't have desires in my captivity.

The one thing I always notice is what Carter doesn't do.

He never kisses me. Never once. And he doesn't talk to me the same way when there are people around. I've met two of his brothers and each time I anticipated being tossed aside or demeaned. But each time, Carter's talked to me as if I'm a friend, maybe. Or a business acquaintance. As do his brothers, although their words are few.

When we're alone, it's different. There's a comfort in his voice I didn't expect that's only replaced by a heavy cadence of desire when he gives me a command.

The combination of all of this is a whirlwind of chaos in my mind.

But one fact remains the same: Another day survived is another day I'm Carter's whore.

My bare feet sink into the rug beneath the bed as I slink off of it and walk toward the cup of coffee on the dresser. It's still hot to the touch.

A million thoughts bombard me every waking moment.

Why is he doing this is the one that's a constant. Carter's a man of intentions. Calculated and manipulative.

Lifting the hot cup of coffee to my lips, I blow across the top and feel the heat caress my face.

He could have slipped something into the cup. He could have left it on the dresser intentionally to remind me of yesterday. My feet are planted right where I was when he punished me.

I go over every possible reason he could have had for putting a cup of a coffee within sight and leaving it for me. It's flavored with enough cream and sugar that the bitter coffee flavor is less evident. Yesterday I made a cup for myself, my first cup of coffee since I've been here. And he must have watched.

Maybe that was the reason he left this here; he wanted me to know he was watching. Maybe he just wanted me to wake up.

Swallowing the sweetened drug, I decide it doesn't matter. I could wonder all I want, but I'll never know.

The only thing that matters is that if I didn't drink it, he would know, and I imagine he would be disappointed. Which is something I don't want to risk happening after yesterday.

I'm determined to be cautious and smart with every decision.

To not go back to the cell, but also to help Carter. I haven't forgotten his deal. He said I would help him and then he'd give me everything. I'm waiting, staying in his good graces.

But something is going to change. I can feel it in my bones. All I have to do is obey and wait for the time to strike. Either for his plan to come to fruition or for another opportunity to make its presence known so I can escape and go back to the safety of my father's home.

Before I even realize it, the ceramic mug is empty in my hands and I leave it on the dresser to change into the clothes he left for me on the end of the bed.

Another routine of his. It's the routines that give me comfort. Knowing what to expect, and how to react. That's something that doesn't frighten me, if nothing else.

The fabric is thicker today. Nothing sheer or delicate. I have to grip the shoulders of it and hold it at arm's length to discover it's a black cotton wraparound dress. It's beautiful and as I slip it on, the soft fabric tickling just above my knee where it stops, I start to feel beautiful myself.

The necklace, the dress. They're classically elegant and hug my curves. I'm tempted to brush my hair and use some of the toiletries Jase bought for me.

More than anything, I want to draw the image of the woman I used to be onto the new canvases I was given last night. A blank page begs to be covered in ink, and I feel and look so different now. Maybe not so much on the surface, but everything I think and feel is no longer a semblance of what once was.

But first, I dress how he wants me to, I'll seek him out,

and then I'll bide my time hiding in the art where I can remember what used to be and hold on to the last piece of the girl I used to know.

I know I'm only playing into Carter's hand as I thread my fingers through my locks and make a braid, placing it over my shoulder and then reach for the cosmetic bag. I don't recognize myself.

But the woman in the mirror is lovely. The kind of lovely that fills other women with envy, but as I drop the mascara onto the counter, I know that no one would envy me and all I am is a pretty fuck doll for Carter.

For now. It's what I have to be. Or at least that's what I tell myself. I try to dignify it by convincing myself that I have to in order to survive. But I can't deny the thought of him commanding me to spread my legs for him sends a wave of heat and want to my core.

Stepping out of the bedroom makes me nervous. It doesn't make much sense to feel safe at all here, but there is a hint of safety in knowing that only Carter will come into his bedroom. I know what to expect. Outside of the confines of those walls are things I have yet to explore.

I know where the den is, and I spent a good bit of time there yesterday. Photographs upon photographs and beautiful art lined every inch of wall in the den. It was easy to lose myself, and take in each one, imagining I had somehow slipped away and fallen into the art, away from here.

Someone in here has a fondness for old trucks. Nearly ten photographs had trucks in them, rusted and worn down, the hoods covered in snow or blue flowers peeking out from under the tires. I've never felt so strongly that old trucks are beautiful until I felt the emotion from the photographs. Maybe I'll draw that instead. Or both. I have plenty of time for both.

I know where the kitchen is from Carter's bedroom too.

And I've ventured there on my own once, but the other times Carter's brought me there.

Yesterday he made me kneel in the kitchen. The way he said it reminded me of the punishment in his bedroom, and I quickly fell to the ground to obey.

The cold floors were smooth and unforgiving against my legs, but I stayed still and at his feet as he fed me bits of his meals. I think he truly enjoys doing it. Having me on my knees beside him and at his mercy. And I have to admit, I didn't hate it, at least not until someone came into the kitchen.

I could hear whoever it was walking in, but they didn't say a word. I remember how I stilled, how I didn't know what to do.

Carter continued to place the chunks of salmon between my lips. And within seconds, whoever had entered, left.

From what I know, there are four men living here. The only other one who's talked to me outside of Carter is Jase. But I imagine it's only when Carter permits it. And I have a mental note in the back of my head to befriend him. The more ammunition I have, the better.

But I'll be careful. I'll be smart. And for now, that means obeying.

I'm nearly to the right threshold of the grand kitchen when I see Carter leaning against the counter, an iPad in his hand and his attention focused on it.

I can't help the way I freeze. As if I could somehow blend into the rich hall and vanish before he could see me.

Even if his touch lights every nerve ending of mine on fire, I still fear Carter. That will never change. Letting out a shaky breath is my downfall; Carter peeks up from his task and sees me. His gaze is lethal as he takes in my appearance.

Slowly. Ever so slowly.

Every inch of skin where his gaze lingers is instantly set ablaze.

"Come." It's the only word I'm given. A command not to be denied, and that rapid hammering in my chest intensifies. One step after another.

My life has become a series of careful steps.

Before I've even come fully into the kitchen, he commands me to kneel and I hesitate. His voice is different. The reverence and desire are absent. Something's wrong and immediately I feel defensive. My hands feel clammy as I wonder what's changed. I nearly swear to him that I haven't done anything wrong.

I've only ever kneeled at his feet, but the power in his

voice makes my knees weak and I drop to the floor where I am, feet away from him in the hall, although I'm afraid he wanted me next to him. Fear. Fear commands these so carefully taken steps.

A moment passes and then another before he glances my way, through the doorway to the kitchen. "Here, songbird. Come kneel here." There's an edge of annoyance in his voice and I nearly cry. It's ridiculous. Utterly ridiculous that his reprimand would upset me to that extent, but as I crawl the last few feet to sit beside him in a kneeling position, my body nearly buckles, and I realize why this morning Carter seems different. Harder and less interested.

"You have her trained well." The man's voice sparks anger in my blood. It mixes with the fear, confusing me and I have a difficult time managing my expression, my movements. Everything in me is screaming to look at Romano, to stare into his cold dark eyes and tell him to go fuck himself.

"There's still plenty for her to learn," Carter speaks absently, swiping the screen of the iPad and focusing his attention on it. He doesn't touch me. Not like he does around his brothers.

My head hangs low, so low it nearly hurts my neck, but I don't want Romano to see my face. I have to bite the inside of my cheek so hard that it bleeds to keep from speaking up.

Be smart, I remind myself although it doesn't soothe a damn thing I'm feeling.

"How's--"

Carter cuts Romano off and states, "I'm happy with it. Let's move forward."

With his simple words, Carter leaves my side to walk the few feet across the kitchen, passing the iPad back to Romano and I chance a peek up. In his crisp dress shirt and dark gray slacks, Carter's expensive, dominating appearance is at odds with Romano's mien. His shirt hangs baggy in the front, not tailored to be fitted, I'd suspect because of his weight.

"When does it begin?" Carter asks with his back to Romano as he stalks toward me. He catches my stare and holds it until he reaches me, forcing me to pull my chin up so I don't break his gaze.

He only looks away when his hand reaches my hair and he cups the back of my head. The satisfaction and thrill of having him hold me so gently and possessively are undeniably fucked up. But still, I nearly smile.

The more comfortable I get, the more I grow to crave his small touches and the warmth of his body.

It's not supposed to be this way, but I can feel myself slipping into this new reality.

"Next week," Romano answers him and I can practically hear his grin. "We'll start taking them out all at once. As many as we can."

Adrenaline pumps in my veins, remembering the conversation from weeks ago. He's going to kill my father's men and all I can think about is Nikolai, my first kiss and only true friend in this world. My family and everyone I grew up with.

I know, and yet I can do nothing. The air around me is suffocating as I sit there silently, remembering how easily some of them have killed before, how I've wished that those men would die so many times. But not all of them. Not my family. Not Nikolai.

Inside I scream at myself to beg for answers, to beg for mercy. But on the surface I stay calm and wait for Romano to leave. There has to be a way for me to spare some of the people I love. The only people I love. The only family I have.

Please, show mercy. I nearly whisper the words as Carter leaves me yet again, walking Romano to the door and leaving me lonely and pathetic on the floor of the kitchen.

I don't make a sound. I stay silent.

But I will beg. I will fight. I will do anything. I won't let them kill my family.

There has to be a way.

If he cares anything for me, he'll show mercy. My gaze drops to the shadows of the two of them in the hall. The saddest part of the last thought is that I already know he won't show mercy. I'm only his whore.

CHAPTER 23

CARTER

The fire crackles. I've always found comfort in the soothing sound. My songbird's humming is the only thing that's come close and whether or not she knows it, she's been humming every so often since I left her in the den.

Gripping the back of the tufted sofa, I watch the glow of the fire play across her face. The shadows only make her look more beautiful. Even though she's drawing near the hearth, she hasn't turned on the lights. The sun set hours ago, taking the daylight that filled this room with it. But she's stayed by the fire, consumed with her art.

"Aria." I attempt to keep my voice calm and gentle, so I don't startle her. But I achieve the opposite and the black charcoal in her hand leaves a mar across the center of the piece she's drawing. Surprise and fear are evident from her parted lips but she shifts her expression quickly, leaving her pad and the charcoal on the hearth to kneel for me.

She doesn't address me any other way, simply waiting for a command. Her submission is beautiful, but there's a twisting in my gut. She's faking it. It's only because of yesterday. She's only being good because I caught her searching through my room. She doesn't fool me.

"You did well this morning," I compliment her as I round the large sofa. Her eyes watch me; they watch every movement I make.

As much as I see her, I know she sees me. It's one of the things that's pulling me to her every second of every day.

I don't want to miss the little hints of honesty that she can't hide from me.

"I don't like that man," she says under her breath, daring to raise her eyes to me. "Romano." A grin pulls at my lips. "I couldn't tell," I say, toying with her.

She did perfectly. Submitting to me and showing him how I have her under my thumb. That I've gained control of her, even when she couldn't contain her contempt for him.

She's helping me set him up for his own demise, and she doesn't even know it.

"Can I tell you a secret?" I ask her as I sink into the sofa, relaxing against it as she nods once and then whispers, "Yes."

"Come here." I pat the seat next to me and watch her

debate on whether she should crawl or stand to get here. Glancing at her right hand, covered in charcoal, she chooses to stand and reach for the towel on the coffee table. She's deliberate in her motions as she quickly cleans her hands and then walks quietly to sit beside me. Only the crackling of the fire occupies the silence.

As she sits, I slip my arm around her waist, pulling her closer, lowering my lips to her ear then nipping her lobe before moving to her neck.

When I'm touching her, she knows exactly how to behave. She loses that constant inner questioning and gives herself to me completely. Letting her breathing quicken and her head fall to the side. She can't hide from me when my hands are on her.

It's a heady feeling I've grown addicted to.

I imagine she doesn't realize how often she touches me. Like now, how she reaches out to my shoulder as I rake my teeth up and down her neck.

Nipping her ear once more and feeling the thrill of her ragged moans deep in my chest, I whisper to her, "I want the man dead."

Her lashes flutter open and as they do, Jase enters the doorway. He hesitates and nearly turns around, but I gesture for him to enter. Time and time again, she seizes up when another person is added to the equation. She forgets how to react and becomes a lost little bird with a broken wing. Stiff in my embrace, she struggles to know where to look as Jase enters.

Slowly she pulls her legs up onto the sofa and bows her head. I know Jase is watching me, but I can't take my eyes away from her.

"You're mine," I tell her in a voice that commands her to look back at me. "You will hold your head up high." Her eyes widen slightly and then follow my fingers as I trace them from her collar down the center of her chest. "How else will they see this?" My pointer intertwines with the necklace and she nods in understanding.

I can feel her heart racing just beyond my touch, but I let the necklace fall into place and turn back to my brother. The judgment and disgust that lingered in his eyes only days ago are gone, replaced now only by curiosity. It's all going better than I'd hoped, even if it has taken longer than I'd planned.

"It's set for next week." As the words register with Jase and he tells me the shipments are coming in early for Romano, I notice how Aria's demeanor changes again.

She already knows too much. As much as I enjoy her presence, she shouldn't be privy to the knowledge of how her father's empire will fall.

"You look lovely tonight," Jase speaks directly to her. Surprise lights up her face as the fire continues to cast shadows over her.

"Thank you," she says, but her voice is soft, too soft and

she clears her throat to repeat herself. "Thank you."

"I admire your art," he adds, and I glance down at the scattering of papers on the floor. Three new ones today, and each more stunning than the last. She's not rushed anymore. She takes her time, and the beauty she creates is captivating. I never expected to feel proud of what I thought was only a distraction.

The thrill rings in my blood. She craves acceptance, protection, and a tenderness that I can't always give her. But my brothers can. Even now as she worries and struggles, his kindness makes her weaker toward me. Each small gesture of acceptance makes her more willing to obey me.

"She's talented." I compliment her as well, although I speak to Jase.

"Thank you," she says again, and the fidgeting stops momentarily, replaced by a calmer demeanor.

"We'll go over the rest tonight," I tell Jase and he takes the cue to leave easily enough. No more of this in front of her. She needs to be perfect for the dinner.

And then everything will change.

"Tonight then," Jase says and nods a goodnight to Aria. A gentle smile flickers on her lips, but she struggles to speak to him in return.

"You're doing so well," I speak to her gently as Jase leaves us. Her hair is soft under my fingers as I push the locks from her face. "Apart from yesterday morning, I mean."

The reminder makes her stiffen, but only until I trail my fingers back to the necklace, the mix of pearls and diamonds strung together on a thin platinum chain. So delicate and breakable, just like her.

"I'm sorry," she apologizes again.

"No, you're not." The words come out with a sternness that's irrefutable. "I expected as much, but you aren't sorry."

"I'm sorry I disappointed you," she says, and the statement sounds genuine, even as she closes her eyes and swallows noticeably. I take in every hint of her features, seeing nothing but sincerity.

"Aria," I tell her as I slip my hand to the nape of her neck, "you haven't disappointed me." My voice is deeper than I intended, laced with the lust I still have for her.

I thought I would grow tired of her but having Aria and playing with her has become my favorite game.

She only sighs at my statement, a soft sound that's a mix of want and need and something else.

I whisper at the shell of her ear, "I can spoil you; this doesn't have to be something you hate."

"I will give you anything," she whispers and those beautiful eyes peer into mine, searching for mercy, "Please don't kill my family."

"I had to pick a side, but they'll both die, Aria. There's no changing that." If I could steal the pain from her, I would.

"You said you wanted him dead. Romano. Why not side

with my father?"

"Do you think your father would spare me, Aria? Do you think he'd allow me to live?" My voice comes out harder with each word, remembering how my life was almost snuffed out by his hands. Her gorgeous eyes turn to dark wells of sadness. She knows the truth about her father, but still, she continues.

"He would," she whispers with hopefulness.

"He wouldn't," I tell her, expecting to be angered by her naivety, but it's only pity for her that I feel. "You need to stay out of this, Aria," I command her, and she nods once, but I can see the pleas written on her face.

"I can't just do nothing," she whispers.

"You must, or you'll leave me with no choice." It's not a threat, but it's full of truth and I pray she behaves. "You're smarter than this. You know how to survive."

"I'll always be a prisoner," she murmurs, and her voice is soft but desperate. Her eyes open and she almost says something. She almost begs or pleads or questions. But she doesn't.

"I want to steal the fight from you," I say the words without thinking, without realizing how honest they are. "I will have all of you, Aria."

It takes a moment for her to respond, and when she does, it's with her eyes closed and her words are laced with pain. "I know you will."

She holds on to that pain so well. Gripping it chaotically, just to hold on to something. In a way, that enrages the very core of my being. But soon all she'll hold on to is me. So soon. I have to be patient with her. If nothing else, time will dull her pain and then all she'll have is me.

"Lie back," I give her the command and she obeys instantly, falling onto the sofa and resting her head on the decorative pillow. Brushing my hand against her inner thigh, she parts her legs for me. The cotton slips up higher, but I have to lift her ass up and push the dress up to her waist to see all of her.

"You're always wet for me," I utter the words beneath my breath as my cock hardens. My fingers trail up and down her shaved pussy. Her lips glisten with arousal and her breathing hitches.

I unbutton my collar and pull my shirt off first, dropping it carelessly to the floor. Every second that passes, Aria's breathing gets heavier. The sofa groans under me as I shift my weight to move my shoulders between her thighs.

Gripping her ass to hold her in place, I start with a single languid lick of her tempting cunt. When I look up and find her lips parted, her eyes wide and her cheeks that beautiful hue of pink, I decide I won't stop licking, sucking and tongue fucking her cunt until she can't fight me any longer.

And then I'll have her writhing under me, cumming on my cock like she was made to do.

CHAPTER 24

ARIA

This isn't what life is supposed to be like. Not for someone like me. Surrounded by luxury and chained to a gilded cage, I shouldn't wake up feeling at ease.

But that's how I feel. I know that so long as I obey Carter, I'll be all right. I'll be safe and pampered even.

While my family is murdered, and I do nothing.

I can't allow it. I won't.

I have to remind myself with each kindness he offers me.

Like last night. I was holding onto a deadly combination of hate and hope. Desperate for a way out of here so I could warn my family, or a way to convince Carter to be on my father's side to present itself.

And I slipped into sleep knowing I needed to do

something. That today I would act and find a way. But each kindness makes me weaker.

I'll never forget the way he held me. Gripping me to him as I lay on my side. My heart raced, and fear was real in my veins. As real as anything else. Sleep still held my eyes tightly shut until I heard his voice, recognized the deep measure of his determined words. "Come back to me." His breath was hot on my neck, his hand strong as it splayed across my belly. He held me so close and so tightly, I couldn't move when I woke up.

I could still feel the drum of my racing heart as he flipped me onto my back and buried his head in the crook of my neck, kissing me ravenously, as if he'd been deprived of it. And I pined for his lips on mine, but he didn't give them to me. I was still blinking away sleep when he whispered, "If you're going to scream a name in your sleep, it'll be my name."

I woke up wondering if it was a dream if he hadn't really taken me from a nightmare and fucked me into a deep sleep of desire. But he was still holding me the way he had when I woke up and there was no denying it was real.

"You stopped humming." Carter's deep voice pierces through my thoughts and I look up at him from the ground beneath his feet. Rolling the black charcoal between my fingers I lie to him, something I know I shouldn't do.

"I'm just thinking about what I'd like to draw next."

He knows my response is a lie. His eyes narrow, but he

allows it. I don't think he wants me to go back to the cell any more than I do. Although part of me wonders if one day he'll start fucking me on that mattress and I'll be confined there.

The only thing that relieves that thought is the knowledge that Carter enjoys others seeing how I've become his. How I obey him while he gives me this freedom. If you can call it that.

My gaze wanders across Carter's office and lands yet again on a bench that doesn't belong. It peeks out from under the bookshelf across from me and it simply isn't supposed to be there.

The wood is old and unfinished, at odds with the dark polished shelves housing beautifully covered books.

The hinges have a hint of rust. I tap the charcoal in my hand against the paper and stare at it. Wondering why Carter would allow it to stay.

"Where did the bench come from?" I ask him on a whim. I haven't asked him anything. Not for a single thing. Nor have I initiated conversation. But if I have any hope of changing his mind about my father, I have to be able to speak up. And it starts right now, with that bench. Craning my neck to look at him over the desk, from where I'm seated on the floor in front of him, I wait for his reaction.

"Bench?" he questions, although I already know that he knows what I'm referring to.

Pointing straight in front of me, I answer him, "It doesn't look like it belongs."

I can hear his chair creak as he leans back, and I know he's debating on telling me something, although I don't know what. It's only an old, beat-up bench.

"Do you want to see what it can do?" he asks me, and the tone of his words catches me off guard. He must sense the hesitation because as he rises and makes his way to the bench, he adds, "It's a safe box."

The charcoal in my hand makes a small thud as it hits the paper and I watch Carter open the lid to what I thought was just an old bench.

"It's bulletproof, and it can only be locked from the inside."

"Someone could just pick it up..." I state my thought absently and he gives me a small, sad smile.

"If they knew you were in there, they could try, although it's heavy. So heavy I couldn't lift it with Daniel the day I got it."

I let my eyes graze over Carter's shoulders then back to what I thought was only a bench. I take a quick breath, ready to ask him if it was from his childhood. It's obviously far too small for him. Although I know I could easily fit. But I don't question him.

"The lock is here," he tells me and fiddles with something inside of it that clinks. I have to stand up to see and since I'm standing, I walk closer to him and to the contraption.

"Is it really safe?" I ask him and he's quiet until I look up at him. His eyes question mine. "As safe as a box can be."

Now that I'm closer to it, I'm certain I could fit inside. It would be tight. As if reading my mind, Carter tells me, "You'd fit. You'd be safe."

My eyes drift to the brass locks on the inside. There are only two, but they travel along the entire top edge. A long rod of steel falls down and slips into place when locked. I imagine you could open it with a welding torch, but with all this metal, the person inside would be burned, scarred, maybe killed before the box would actually open.

"Can you breathe in there?" I whisper my question.

Carter nods and runs his finger along small slits in the box, designed so they can't be seen from the outside, but light filters through them.

I swallow thickly as Carter places a hand on my lower back and asks, "Do you want to get inside?"

I should say no, the fear inside of me is there at the forefront, screaming that the small space is dangerous. It may look like safe, but the cell was much larger, and it was instrumental in my downfall.

But the fear is so minuscule. So quiet. It's hard to be scared of something so... insignificant when my life is in the hands of a man like Carter. And I think he'd like it if I got inside.

I nod once and as I do, I'm already lifting my right leg. With Carter's hand to balance me, I slip inside easily.

"The locks are here, but you'll have to feel for them when the lid is shut, it'll be dark."

"Are you going to close it?" I ask him and my heart pounds.

I don't want him to leave me here. He towers over me and answers, "You'd be the one to close and lock it, Aria."

"Right. Of course," I say then shake my head and reach for the lid. As if it's the obvious thing to do. It strikes me then as odd that he would grant me this, a safe place to be away from him. But I could only stay in here so long.

This box is meant for hiding. The thought occurs to me as I lower the lid. It's meant to hide, to stay quiet and not be seen.

My heart thumps once as the lid shuts tightly and a tiny ray of light shines through. It's filtering in through a small slit. One that can't be seen from the outside, but I can see it clearly.

My fingers trace the locks as they slip into place, a heavy thump from the steel rod falling causing my body to react by bucking back.

Thump, thump. My heart hammers.

It reminds me of the door being kicked in when I was hiding in the closet.

My throat closes and my eyes water as I clearly see my mother through the slit. Just like I did when I hid in the closet. The memory is vivid. It's too real.

"Stop!" I scream and struggle against the lid. Panic consumes me. *I can't stay here, I can't be quiet and let him murder her.*

Screams rip through my throat. "Stop it!" I scream and it's only then that I hear Carter.

His fists pound above me.

The tears that stream down my face seem to burn my skin as I fumble for the locks.

"Carter, please!" I beg him.

"Lift the locks!" he yells at me, but I can't. I can't see them. All I can see is him holding my mother down, stabbing her over and over. The blood was everywhere. He was too fast. I couldn't save her.

"Please," I beg him and feel the entire box lift from the ground only to fall hard on the floor beneath me. Jostling me and reminding me where I am.

"Open it, Aria!" he yells at me and I try to find the locks. It takes me a long moment. Each second, images of my mother pass before my eyes. The way she tried to fight him. The way she tried not to scream. I know she didn't want me to hear or to see.

But you can only hide so much.

Finally, the locks slip back into place in my shaking hand and the mechanism opens with a loud thunk. Carter practically rips the top open. His strong arms pull me up and I'm safe in the light of the office. The images fade and I find myself huddled in his arms, feeling foolish and unable to explain what happened. My body won't stop shaking.

I hate the box. I hate it. I hate it more than the cell.

"Shhh," he shushes me and brings me to his chair. I think he's going to set me down in it, but he doesn't. He keeps holding me tight in his arms. My body shudders and I wish I could calm myself down and take it all back.

I can't stop crying.

I haven't had a panic attack in so long. It's only been night terrors for years.

"I'm sorry," I mumble the words and brush my tears away furiously. They're hot and I can already feel my eyes becoming puffy. I can hardly breathe.

"I hate the box," I push the words out as if I could blame it.

"It's okay." Carter's answer is soothing. He doesn't ask what happened. He doesn't push me for anything.

He only holds me and comforts me, running his hand up and down my back. His warmth and strength and scent surround me. And I want more of it.

I would die for more of it.

A knock at the office door startles me. "Hush, songbird," Carter whispers against my hair before calling to the door, "Come in."

It's Jase. It's almost always Jase.

He stands in the doorway, gripping the knob and not letting it go. I get the sense that he doesn't like to stay when I'm around. Like if I wasn't here, he'd have taken a seat. A shudder runs through my body, and I bury myself deeper into Carter's arms, wishing I could go back to just a minute ago.

"I just wanted to let you know, the dinner is set to go as planned."

Seeing Jase, reminds me of everything once again. Like being woken from a deep sleep. Back to realizing all of this is wrong and there isn't a piece of it that should feel right.

Back to the fact that I'm nestled in the arms of the man who's set to destroy everything I am.

The thought of dying for more of Carter's touch is still vibrant in my mind. And it withers like the petals of a broken flower in the scorching heat as the sane side of me remembers what I really am and who he really is.

"He's coming?" Carter asks and there's a deep rumble of anger hidden beneath his words. It's enough of an edge that my body stills in his embrace.

Jase nods, his gaze moving from me to Carter. "He's coming."

"And are we still on for tonight?" Carter asks Jase in a tone quite different. A tone that makes me curious. Curious enough to peek at Jase.

Jase's gaze flickers to me again before he answers, "Yeah, we're on for tonight." Patting the doorframe, he nods toward Carter and leaves us alone.

The tears, the flashback, and panic, they seem foolish now. It was only a glimpse at the past. Carter loosens his hold on me as my body stiffens and I hold my arms to my chest.

Why does he hold me and comfort me, when I'm nothing to him but a play toy? It's so he can make me weak. I know that's why. I'll fall powerless to him so easily. And he'll use me up and throw me out.

I can already see it happening.

"I'll be gone tonight." Carter's voice seems deeper, rougher even. The sound forces me to look at him as he speaks. It's odd to be at nearly eye level as I sit on his lap.

His gaze is so sharp, I can barely look him in the eye.

"You can get yourself dinner. And wait for me in either the kitchen, den, or bedroom." I stare at the knob on one of the drawers of his desk, nodding my head in obedience and feeling awkward and too afraid to speak.

My body shudders as he lays a hand on my upper back, between my shoulder blades and working his way down to the small of my back.

"Maybe you need a drink?"

When I turn to him this time, I want to yell at him. I want to hide. I want to cry.

The question is on the tip of my tongue, *why are you doing this to me?*

But I already know the answer. It's why Carter does everything.

Because he can. Because he wants to.

CHAPTER 25

CARTER

The Red Room wasn't my idea. It was Jase's, of all people. He's quiet, keeps to himself, but he created a club that's the perfect cover-up and a successful business at that. He always stays in the back, where other business is conducted, but nonetheless, Jase's creation is something he's proud of. And every time I come here, I'm reminded of that fact.

The music thrums in my veins before the large red glass doors even open. In a gray tailored suit, I don't exactly blend in with the nightlife. Not like Jase does in his faded jeans and crisp, button-down, open at the collar.

I prefer a suit. Jase prefers to blend in. Each method has its advantages.

"Welcome back, sirs," Jared greets us as we step into the

club, the music at full volume and the smells of alcohol and sex appeal hit me instantly. With the dark red paisley wallpaper that lines the walls and black chandeliers hanging from the sixteen-foot-high black ceiling, The Red Room looks like a nightclub of sin at first glance.

As the alcohol pours throughout the night and the bodies grind against one another, sin is an accurate description. The money flows as easily as the liquor.

Walking past the grinding bodies and kitten eyes from several women holding drinks in one hand and their clutches in another, I ignore it all, listening intently to what Jared has to say.

I stopped everything to come down here with my brother. All because Jared, the club manager, and head of business while we're away, said he had a girl who would talk.

"You sure it's her?" Jase asks him.

"Yeah," Jared nods as we pass the second bar and make our way around the edge of the dance floor to get to the backroom. "She comes in every week asking for it."

"What'd you tell her?"

"Nothing. Just that the delivery is on a delay." The DJ starts a new set and the dance floor roars so loudly the ground shakes as the steel doors to the backroom push open and then close softly, finally silencing the distractions of the club.

"Thanks for waiting for us," Jase tells the two men in the back of the room. Mick is one of them; I don't know the name of the other, but Jase does. This is Jase's place to run. Everyone knows him, and he knows everyone, so I let him lead and stay quiet.

Quiet is dangerous, and that's exactly how I want them to see me.

"Of course, Mr. Cross," Mick says and nods his head at Jase then quirks a smile at me as he adds, "and Mr. Cross."

The small girl seated at the lone table in the room grips the plastic cup of a pink drink that's probably got just as much sugar in it as alcohol. Her lips part open with a hint of disbelief and then she licks them, smiling although it's thin and withered. Just like the state of her body under the too-tight tube top.

"You're waiting for the delivery?" Jase asks, looking to the left and right as if he doesn't want to say it out loud and get caught by someone. I'd laugh at him and his display, but he's damn good at what he does, and I do enjoy a good show.

The girl imitates him, looking over her shoulders at the two hired men of ours in The Red Room t-shirts and black jeans before she nods. "You guys have the best sweets."

"Sweets?" I ask, and she grins at me like she knows a secret she can't wait to tell me.

"It's what the streets are calling it now," she says and bites down on her lower lip, letting her body sway. Jase and I pull out our chairs across from her, the legs scraping across the floor. Sweets. Plural. Because that fucker Romano has his version out. I keep the small hint of friendliness firmly in place. But I'm nothing but pissed at the reminder

"Sweet Lullaby, you mean?" Jase asks, lifting an eyebrow. And again, she nods.

"You're buying a lot of this stuff," Jase tells her although it comes out a question. Her nails scratch down her arms as she glances all around us. She's jittery and the chair legs beneath her keep rasping on the floor.

"I just need it, okay?" Her words are rushed. The air changes around her instantly.

Noting her hollow cheeks, dead eyes, and pale lips, the humor, and vibe that she's down to have a good time have vanished.

"Is it really what you need?" Jase asks and leans forward to stare into her eyes. "'Cause we've got some other stuff you might want?"

She's in need of a hit. That's for damn sure and if I had to guess her drug of choice is heroin. Maybe coke.

"I just need to grab it and get back," she answers, but her voice is breathy and uncertain. I wait a moment, glancing at Jase as we both hear her swallow over the muted sound of the music playing in the club.

"I think we have some coming, sorry about the wait, miss...?"

"Jenny. Jenny Parks," she answers him and then reaches into her purse for her phone. The two men behind us make a move for their guns, and the little blonde doesn't even notice.

"Fuck, it's already past nine," she says and her face crumples with a mix of anxiety and fear.

As she slips her thumb into her mouth to chew on her nail, Jase asks her, "Hey, is there anything I can get you while you wait?"

"Anything to calm you down a little? Another drink or something stronger?" I add.

Her breath comes out harder. "Yeah, maybe," she replies as her eyes dart from me to Jase. "I just wanted to come in and get the stuff. It'll be here soon?" she asks again, looking down at the phone to check the time. "Like, how soon."

"It could be a bit," Jase says and shrugs, looking at Mick and she watches him shrug too. "We've got other stuff while you wait," he offers but she's already shaking her head, still biting that thumbnail.

She speaks over the finger in her mouth. "I need the sweets first."

The problem with a junkie is that they have a one-track mind. They want the drug. And it's obvious that she gets hers when she delivers our drug to the real buyer.

Jase shrugs again. "An hour, maybe?" He glances at me and I nod my head.

"Fuck," she mutters and cradles her face in her hands.

"You want us to drop it off somewhere else?" Jase asks, and she peeks up through her lashes. We're getting the address of where this product is going. Either from her telling us or from us following her. Whatever the fuck we have to do.

"I have to get back. I'm sorry," she rushes her words as she slides her phone off the table and into her purse.

"We can get you something to take the edge off while it comes in and we can talk a little?" Jared suggests to her from where he's standing guard by the steel doors. She seems to get it then. The reality of what's going on hits her like a ton of bricks and she's shit at hiding it.

"It's just... it's my brother. You know? He needs it, and he doesn't like me to be late."

"Your brother?" Jase questions and I glance at Mick, standing behind the seated blonde, who shakes his head once. Little Jenny doesn't have a brother.

"Yeah, and he doesn't like people to come around, you know?" Again, her words are rushed and she looks at the men behind her then at us.

"I can just come back another time," she mumbles. Her breathing is sporadic as she pulls her purse to her chest.

She takes a second to stand up, but Mick's hand on her shoulder makes her pause.

A second drops between us all, heavy with the consequences of what's to come.

She's buying for someone else and lying to cover it up. Someone who keeps her doped up and someone who scares her enough to give her the strength to resist her next hit from us.

Her head turns slowly so she can see Mick's large hand gripping tighter onto her shoulder. The fear that drifts from her is palpable and sickening.

"You tell your brother we're sorry we couldn't get it to him tonight, Jenny," Jase speaks up and instantly Mick's grip on the girl loosens.

I can practically hear her heart beating as she looks at Jase wide-eyed. She's frozen still until he leans back in his seat and tells her with a wink, "We'll have it for you next time."

"You let us know if you want to talk anytime now, you hear me?" Jared says as he opens the door to the club and the music flows into the small back room.

Jenny nods her head furiously, stumbling into the empty chair next to her before taking off out of the room without another look back.

"Follow her," I tell Mick and with a single nod he's gone. Jase's blunt nails tap against the table as the door closes and the sound of the nightlife beyond it is muted once again.

"You let her off easy," I say quietly under my breath.

"Girls don't need to be dragged into this shit." That's his only answer and he doesn't bother to lower his voice like I did.

The same table he's tapping, I've covered with blood in the past. It wouldn't have come to that with the blonde, but a little lie to get her talking wouldn't have hurt her. Showing our cards that we know she's buying for someone else, well that might have gotten a word or two from her. Maybe a name.

"Maybe he's sending girls because he knows you're weak for them," I suggest. All of us have our limits. And women happen to be the common thread between us.

"Fuck you, I'm not weak," he tells me although I can see him considering it. It's in his eyes.

The corners of my lips tip up into a smirk as Jared lights up a cigarette. But with a puff and the words that come out of his mouth, the smile vanishes. "With the Talvery girl shit, they should know we aren't pussies when it comes to women."

The silence stretches in the room for a moment with neither of us commenting.

"The Talvery girl," I say beneath my breath and it gets a comment from Jared, but I don't bother to listen to him. "She's mine," I tell him, cutting off his joke or whatever the fuck was coming out of his mouth.

I stand abruptly, letting an anger I haven't felt in a long time dictate my words. Staring into Jared's eyes, the words rip from my mouth, "The next time someone refers to her as that, *the Talvery girl*," I practically spit out the name, "you tell them, she's all mine."

My teeth grind against each other so hard, I swear they'll crack.

Jared doesn't speak, doesn't move. I don't think he's breathing, although the cigarette in his mouth stays oddly still with the glow of amber making his expression look even paler.

My muscles coil, waiting for him to call her that again.

She's not *the Talvery girl*. She doesn't belong to them.

"What's her name?" I ask him, tilting my head and that cigarette wavers in his mouth. "Take out the fucking cigarette and tell me what the fuck her name is." My eyes pierce into his as he drops the cigarette from his mouth, barely catching it between his fingers and swallowing thickly. The cords of his neck are tight, and I can hear him swallow.

"I—I—" he stutters, and I lean in closer to scream in his face, the words of my question scratching and ripping their way up my throat, "What's her name?"

"I don't know," he says in a quavering admission.

"It's Aria," I say then pat his shoulders with both of my hands as he struggles to look me in the eyes. The anger wanes as I feel his sweat beneath my hands.

"It's Aria, and she doesn't belong to the Talverys anymore." My words are calm, eerily so.

"Of course, she doesn't," Jared shakes his head slightly, his lips turning into a hesitant smile. "She's yours. Aria is yours and she's called Aria."

He won't shut the fuck up, the poor prick.

"You let anyone who calls her otherwise know," I tell him, nodding my head once toward a spot on the brick wall. The bricks are redder, newer and don't blend in.

"I'd hate to lose it and have to blow some fucker's poor skull open because he pissed me off."

"Yeah," Jared's answer is a whisper of fear. "Aria, and

she's yours."

Jase's hand hitting the back of my shoulder is the only thing that rips my gaze away from Jared's.

"Keep up the good work, Jared." Jase adds, "Good job tonight," and pushes the door open to go back out into the bar.

He holds it open for me and I move around Jared, still very much stuck in his place and only nodding his response as if he's scared to speak. As I take a step to leave, I glance down at him, the disgusting smell of piss overriding the scent of cigarettes. The fucker pissed himself.

I wish I could smile or feel any sense of pleasure from knowing how deeply rooted the fear goes. But all I can think is that these assholes are calling my Aria, *the Talvery girl.*

She's so much more than that.

"You've got to back down with that," Jase tells me as we walk side by side through the club. There's no one around us that could hear, but still, I want to tell him to fuck off.

"I don't have to do shit," I respond in a grunt, the rage still looming, but even as the words are spoken, I know he's right. They could use her against me. She could so easily become known as my weakness.

"What's the point of doing that?" he asks me, cutting off my train of thought.

But I don't have an answer ready. There's always a reason. Everything I do has a purpose. It takes the entire walk through the club for me to respond, and not until we're out of the front doors where the cool air greets us, and the moonlight lingers over the parking lot.

The wind whips against my face, and Jase slips his hands into his pockets as the valet pulls our car up to the curb. "The point is that they've forgotten she's mine when they call her a Talvery. I won't have anyone forget she belongs to me."

Chapter 26

Aria

Carter had me drink a glass of whiskey with orange bitters but somehow it tasted like chocolate. I don't know what it was exactly, but it's still humming through me. He left me with a second drink in his office and it's the second one that did this to me.

Even as I stand in the kitchen, busying myself with something to take my mind off everything that's going on around me, I can feel the alcohol numbing the pain. As if I'm spared from what's going to happen, and it's everything else that's moving. I'm just standing here.

But I hate it. I don't want to be helpless and beg for mercy from a man who won't show it. I don't want to seem helpless, but I have no choice.

The refrigerator is full of nearly anything I could want. Fresh eggs, deli meat, fruits, and vegetables. Most of the meats for dinner are frozen, but there's plenty to satisfy me.

I'm not hungry in the least, but Carter told me to eat and so here I am.

It took me a while to get started, long after Carter had left.

Instead of doing anything at all, I stared at the door. And then each of the windows I passed. And the windows to the garden. I wish I could leave and tell my father they're coming, but I'm sure he knows. That's the only comfort I have in this powerless state. My father must know they're coming for him.

The knife slices through a tomato. It's so sharp the skin splits instantly without any pressure at all. I suck the taste of the whiskey from my teeth. I can't do anything, but I need to do something.

The thunk of the knife on the cutting board is the only thing I hear over and over again.

"What are you making?" A deep voice from behind me makes me jump. The knife slips from my hand and I'm too scared to jump away from it as it crashes to the floor. I stand there breathless with anxiety shooting through my veins.

"Shit," the voice says as my heart races and pounds in my chest.

It's Daniel. I've seen him before and I know that's his name. But he hasn't said a word to me. He never even looks at me. Yet, now I'm alone with him, and Carter's nowhere to be seen. In dark jeans and a black t-shirt, he runs his hand through his hair with a shameful look on his face. "I should've come from the other direction, huh?" There's a sweetness about him, but I don't trust him. I don't trust any of the Cross brothers.

"I'm just keeping an eye on you," Daniel says easily, and his lips quirk up into a half smile. "A salad?" he asks.

"Yeah," I say, but my answer is a whisper. It's odd to be a prisoner yet remain free to move about. Even odder to have a conversation with someone as if there's nothing at all wrong with my position.

I force myself to swallow and bend down slowly, keeping him in my periphery, to pick up the knife. My body trembles as I turn my back to him just enough to walk to the sink and rinse it off. "Avocado, tomato and Italian dressing. I was craving something like it," I tell him as the water pours down onto the sharp edge of the knife. The light reflects in the water and my heart thumps again.

"Salt tooth?" he asks me, and I nod, eyeing him but trying to just have a conversation. I wonder what he thinks of me. What he thinks of Carter for keeping me here.

All I can look at is the knife in my hand, the alcohol is thrumming, my nerves are high, and I don't know how to survive anymore.

The idea of an escape plan is forming, but the anxiety is so much higher.

His footsteps give him away as he walks to the other side of the counter, closer to where the chunks of avocado and freshly cut tomato wait for me. My mind is highly aware of where he is. And who he is.

He knows how to get out of here. He could be my ticket to freedom.

"Did you find the bowls?" he asks me as I turn around to face him, the knife feeling heavier in my hand.

With the water off, the room is silent. Eerily so. Or maybe it's just because of the thoughts running through my mind. The counter is hard against my lower back as I lean against it to keep me steady as I watch him open a cabinet and pull out a bowl.

He smiles at me like he's my friend or my companion, and not a guard to keep me here. And he lets me hold the knife. He doesn't even look at it. I have a weapon and I'm a prisoner here, yet he doesn't care in the least. *Why would he, you weak girl?* the voice in the back of my head taunts me and laughs.

"Thank you," I say, and my voice sounds small and weak. Gripping the countertop behind me, it feels so cold, so unforgiving in comparison to how hot my body is right now.

The ceramic bowl clinks as it hits the countertop and Daniel smiles at me. A handsome, charming smile with his hands up in the air as he says, "I'm not going to hurt you; I promise."

I'm the one with the knife.

I keep thinking it as I take each small step toward the counter.

My bare feet pad on the cold floor.

I offer him a small smile, but I don't say anything and neither does he.

Until that knife slices so easily through the tomato again. I imagine the way it would go down, but it's hard to focus. I couldn't kill him. He'd have to push in the code and then I'd run.

"Is he treating you alright?" he asks me, and my grip tightens on the knife. He could so easily push in a code and grant me freedom. And then I could tell my father they're coming.

Raising my eyes to his for the first time, I ask him, "What do you think?" I'm surprised by the strength, but I crave more of it.

His gaze flickers to the door behind me and then back to me.

Silence descends upon the kitchen.

"He's in a difficult position," Daniel offers me when I start to cut the slices into chunks, trying not to think of what would happen if I failed. What Carter would do to me if I tried to escape and failed. My chest hollows and my stomach drops at the thought. The cell. Or worse, the box. He knows what that box would do to me if he put a lock on the outside of it.

My blood runs cold.

"He's not a bad man," Daniel says, and I watch as the knife in my hand trembles as it hovers over the remaining slices.

Bad man? He's not a bad man? If only Daniel knew what

I was thinking.

"Good men don't do what he's done," I tell Daniel without looking at him. "I begged him last night to spare my father. My family," I say and my voice cracks.

"I'm sorry, but you know he can't do that." It's his only response and I crumble inside. My heart twists in a painful way. It's a horrible ache that I can't explain when I hear Daniel turn to walk away.

He's leaving me. Because he can. Because it doesn't matter if he leaves me to wallow all alone. All I'll ever be is alone and pathetic if I don't even try.

My fingers wrap around the knife until my knuckles are white and I cry out for him. "Daniel!" His tall, lean body stiffens, the muscles in his shoulders rippling as he turns around.

He's maybe five feet from me. But the kitchen island separates the two of us.

Be smart, I remind myself. But at this point, nothing I'm about to do is smart. Lowering the knife to my side, the blade nearly caresses my skin when I clear my throat.

"I'm sorry," I offer him although I can hardly hear myself over the furious pounding of my heart in my chest. "Could you show me where the seasonings are?" I have to swallow before I can add, "Please."

Daniel's mouth is set in a grim straight line; his eyes pierce deeply into me like he knows exactly what I'm about to do. But he walks toward me. He walks to my side of the island.

Inside I'm screaming that it's a trap, that he knows. My blood rushes in my ears and the sweat from my hand nearly makes the knife slip.

Five feet becomes four, becomes three, becomes two.

And he turns his back to me, reaching at eye level to open a cabinet before turning around and finding that knife pointed at his throat.

The sweat that crawls along my skin is sickening. It covers every inch of me as I try to speak, but my dry throat won't allow it.

Stupid girl! I hear the voice yell at me. Regret and fear are instant, but the knife is in the air and I can't take it back. My hand feels as if it's shaking, but the knife is steady.

I can't go back. "Get me out of here," I breathe as he stares at me with disdain.

"You don't want to do this, Aria." Daniel's words are so genuine, so sincere, that I almost regret taking the step forward and nearly pressing the blade to his throat.

"I want to leave." I somehow push the words out. How strong they sound, although I'm panicked.

Daniel's eyes turn sympathetic, or maybe they just look back at me as if I'm the pathetic one. I can't tell. He deceives me so.

"I can't help you with that." My heart plummets and races at the same time. This is my only chance, my only hope.

"Open the front door." As I give the command, I step

forward and my trembling hand pushes the knife closer to him, slicing the skin of his upper neck, just slightly. A small nick, but it cuts him. *I cut him.*

The horror of seeing the bright red blood distracts me for a moment, a moment long enough for Daniel to shove his hand in front of me and try to grip the knife.

He may be fast, but my fear is faster. The knife pierces through his shirt and bicep, easily cutting into him, slicing his arm as I stumble back.

My heart beats so hard I swear I'll die from terror alone.

The hot grip of his hand burns into my forearm even after he's let go. My back hits the counter and I jump slightly, but I keep the knife up and sidestep slowly around him. The adrenaline is higher than I've ever felt before.

This is bad, my heart screams in terror, *this is fucking bad*. And I've lost the advantage of surprise, the threat of the knife minuscule compared to what it was a moment ago.

"Let me go!" I yell at him as he seethes at me. His grimace grows to something else. Something that looks hurt for me once again. And I want to sneer at him and his pity, but I feel sorry for me too. And there's nothing lower than that.

"I said let me go!" I'm too afraid to get closer to him and every step feels like my knees may give out from the pure adrenaline pumping through me.

"Even if I opened the door, there are two guards at the gates and I'm not leaving anytime soon. They know that."

His voice is stern, and he takes his eyes from me to look at the cut. "Damn, you got me good," he says, still not even bothering to look at me. As if I'm not a threat.

"You could hide me in your car." My voice skips over my words as I struggle to think about the next step.

"And be scared of your knife that's with you in my trunk?" he asks and my head sways. My body threatens to sway with it. I failed. I already know I've failed.

Stupid girl, the voice says, but even she pities me and the earlier anger from her is absent.

My heart sinks and it doesn't stop like it's in a never-ending free fall even though I can already feel it in the pit of my stomach. "Get me out of here, please. You can get me out of here," I say although my voice cracks and I take a step forward with the knife. "Please," I beg him.

He finally glances up at me and says, "Put the knife down." That's all he says, in that disinterested tone that all of the Cross brothers seem to have. A tone that's utterly dismissive.

"Fuck you," I almost cry as I tell him off. I have to step closer to him, I have to go through with this. He nearly got the knife from me last time and if he does this time, I'm going back to the cell. Fuck. My throat closes in on itself.

As if hearing my thoughts, Daniel tells me, "I could grab my gun, Aria, don't make me."

His words kill the last bit of hope. What would I do? Throw the knife at him if he ran to get his gun? "Put the knife down."

"Please don't," I plead with him. Tears prick my eyes at how stupid I am. At what's to come.

The cell. I'll be in the cell tonight. And for however long it takes for Carter to let me out after.

The heavy knife feels heavier and I want to point it at myself. A very big part of me thinks I could get farther if I would threaten to hurt myself. But I don't want to be in pain. "Please help me," I barely get the weak words out.

Daniel's response is immediate, his steps deliberate and powerful. My body shakes as he comes close enough to grip the knife, but this time when he wraps his hand around my forearm, I loosen my grip and the knife falls from my hand to his other hand and only then does he let me go.

I cower like a disobedient child or worse, a dog who knows he's about to be beaten.

Silent tears fall, and I wipe them as I listen to the knife drop into the sink before Daniel turns on the faucet to clean his cut. The cut I gave him.

"I'm sorry." My words are choked, and I try to repeat them again but fail. My breathing comes in shallow pants. "I can't go back. Please, I can't."

"Hey, it's okay." Daniel's voice is soft as he approaches me, but fear is the only thing I have to give him until he says, "We don't have to tell Carter."

His words make me stare into his dark eyes. They're

so like Carter's. But the heat and desire aren't there. Just sincerity.

"I won't tell him, okay?" His comforting voice soothes the fear in me. "This will stay between us." The relief that replaces the anxiety nearly makes me throw up.

"Why would you do that?" I question him. "I hurt you."

"Because I would have done the same." His simple answer is comforting, but it doesn't give me any hope.

"I'm sorry," I mumble my apology and have to clear my throat. I'm choking on my words. "I didn't want to... to hurt you."

"Why'd you have to do that?" I shake my head, wiping under my eyes. He adds, "I would have done it, but I thought you were smarter than that."

"I'm sorry." It's all I can say. "I need to get out of here," I insist, and my words bleed with despair.

"It's better that you're here," he tells me. "You're not safe at your father's and I know Carter may not seem like the best person to you right now, but I know there's a reason for all of this."

"My father." The words tumble from my lips. *I'm failing him.*

"You need to eat," Daniel says, backing away from me and not acknowledging me. It's the same thing Carter told me. I just need to eat. And obey.

"You're going to kill him," I say and it's a statement, not a question. I can't even think about eating. The thought is repulsive.

Daniel opens the fridge and ignores me, although he angles his body so he can see me in his periphery.

He closes the door to the fridge with his elbow as he twists off the top to a beer and takes a quick swig, making the dampened shirt of blood glisten in the light and that bit of red on his throat stare back at me.

I almost tell him I'm sorry, yet again. Even with knowing his plans for my father. It's a sickening feeling to not know what's right and wrong, but regardless, you have no choice.

The bottle smacks down on the counter and he finally answers me. "It was going to happen whether or not we stepped in."

"What was?" I ask him in a hushed voice, cautiously, barely raising my eyes to meet his gaze. The only thing I keep thinking is that I need to be nice to him, so he doesn't tell Carter.

"War."

The one-word answer forces my gaze to the polished tile floor. It's quiet while he drinks, and I clean up the mess of the cubed vegetables I won't eat.

"You won't tell Carter?" I feel selfish for daring to bring it back up, but I need to know he won't. If Carter were here for that... I can't even begin to think of what he would do.

"Look at me," Daniel's voice beckons and I do as he tells me. "I am not going to say a word to Carter. Not one word." His voice is soothing, but I find it hard to be anything close to being okay.

"Thank you," I tell him and press my hand to my face to cool it down.

He finishes the beer, all the while I stare at the spot on the floor until I turn instinctively at the sound of his name being called out by a feminine voice.

"Shit," he says under his breath. He's quick to grab me by the arm. His grip is tight, demanding and catches me off guard with that fear returning and spiking through me.

"Go to the den," he demands beneath his hushed breath and attempts to push me out of the kitchen from the other threshold. My feet slip across the floor as he pushes me toward the den.

"Daniel?" the voice calls out again, this time closer and he urges through clenched teeth, "Go."

My shoulders hunch forward and I feel like nothing. Like absolutely nothing. Worthless, pathetic and a weak thing to be pushed around at anyone's whim.

"Don't do it again, Aria. You're smarter than that," he tells me before turning his back to me and walking briskly to the other side of the kitchen.

His words numb me for a moment, even though my feet move of their own free will.

I'm supposed to be smarter than that. Maybe I used to be, but a mix of desperation and the feeling of falling into a dark abyss is all I can see anymore... that mix is deadly to any semblance of intelligence that I have.

My hands tremble and I struggle to breathe, but I try to remember Carter's words from what seems like so long ago. I try to remember what he said that made me feel like I had hope. I try, and I fail.

It doesn't matter what they were. Everything is insignificant when there's nothing you can do to change your fate.

And now that I've been so fucking stupid, he's going to put me back in the cell.

I shouldn't have done that. A heavy breath nearly suffocates me. I need to listen.

With my eyes closed, I whisper, "Daniel won't tell him." But the words have little mercy on my pain, because I know I won't be able to hide it from Carter. He sees me. He sees all of me. And he watches everything.

"What the hell did you do?" A woman's voice carries through the kitchen with shock and worry, startling me and cutting through my thoughts. As quietly as I can, I slink to the side of the doorway, so I can listen but won't be seen.

I didn't know another girl was here. But the way she's talking to Daniel make it obvious that she's with him. Not a prisoner of him. Jealousy and fear mix inside of me and I don't know why I'm so scared of being seen by her. Maybe the trickle of shame as I grip the doorway is indication enough.

"I was drinking and cutting up shit and I thought it would be cool to toss the knife." I hear Daniel give an excuse that's not at all believable. But the girl believes him.

"You could have killed yourself," she reprimands him, although her voice carries a tinge of disbelief. Guilt seeps into my blood. And a part of me knows it's ridiculous to feel sorry for trying to save myself. But so is all of this.

Daniel chuckles. "Of all the ways to die, I don't think it's going to be this, Addison." I can hear him take a drink before telling her, "I got you a beer." I almost walk away, but Addison's next words keep me planted where I am.

"We need to talk." The severity of her tone is sharp.

"Not right now." Daniel talks to her differently than the way he talks to me. Differently than the way Carter talks to me. There's an edge of comfort in his voice and I don't expect it.

"It's always not right now," she responds. "Something's going on." Her tone softens, pleading with him. "Why can't I leave?" she asks him with desperation clinging to every word.

"It's just better to be safe," he replies so lowly I hardly hear him. The thrumming of curiosity flows through me. She can't leave either?

A moment passes and another, I can't see what's going on and I inch forward, hoping to get a peek before the conversation continues. Hoping to see this woman.

"You don't need to know," Daniel says firmly and with that I creep around the corner to see Daniel leaning against the stove. I see him and a beautiful girl around my age shaking her head so hard that her dark wavy hair falls around her shoulders. She covers her face as she gasps, "You keep lying to me." Pain is etched into her ragged voice.

Daniel makes a weak attempt to wrap his arms around her before she pushes him away, his ass hitting the stove and she leaves the kitchen, heading back the way she came. Small sounds of her crying linger behind her. Daniel opens a large drawer that blends into the cabinet and he drops the empty beer bottle and cap into the trash, with a wretched pain in his expression that tears at my own heart.

As he turns to leave, I creep further back into the kitchen, but he hears me and peeks over his shoulder.

Not hiding his pain and then leaving me to mine.

CHAPTER 27

CARTER

I checked the bedroom first. The depraved side of me hoped she would be waiting for me, already warming my bed.

But it was empty.

The den was next, after assuming I'd see her drawing on the floor of the hearth like she enjoys doing.

But the fire wasn't burning, and the room was silent.

Then the kitchen. The empty fucking kitchen. My teeth grit as I pull up the security monitor and cycle through the cameras.

My pulse races and I can hardly see straight as the monitor flickers from one to the next, each proving to be useless in showing me where my Aria is.

I told her to wait for me in the kitchen, den, or bedroom. Those were the only rooms she was permitted to be in, yet my obedient Aria isn't in a single one of them.

My heart pounds and my temperature rises.

She didn't get away.

I only left for three hours. Just enough time to drive to the club for the meet and then back. Daniel was watching her. I have to remind myself that she's still here somewhere as the cameras loop back around to the beginning.

"Fuck!" My anger gets the best of me, but as I spit out the word and feel the tension in my shoulders and chest rise, I both see and hear her at the same time.

The wine cellar in the corner of the kitchen passed in a blur on the screen the first time, but there she is, in the corner, cross-legged with a bottle in her lap. And the sweet sound of her humming travels through the kitchen.

I walk quietly to the cracked door, only a sliver of light shining into the kitchen.

Listening to the cadence of her soft voice, her humming rises and a word slips out, but I don't recognize the song. The melody is somber, somewhat melancholy.

I inch closer, careful to be quiet and slip the door open as a bottle clinks against the tile floor, notably empty judging from the hollow sound.

Aria's dark locks fall back away from her face and chest as she lays her head back against the wall, her nose pointed toward the ceiling as she hums a little louder.

It's addictive, listening to those sweet sounds. Her voice

has always captivated me and I suppose it always will. What saves you from the darkness is something extraordinary.

"This isn't the kitchen," I say and break up her melody. The green and amber colors swirl into a deadly concoction of fear in her gaze as she takes in my words. I watch her throat as she swallows; I can practically hear her tense breathing as she seats herself in a kneeling position to tell me, "I didn't know."

She still doesn't look at me when she speaks. Sometimes in the evenings, she'll peek at me. But she doesn't like to look me in the eye.

Her cotton blouse is loose and baggy, offering me a glance down her shirt, although her hair lays in the way as it hangs in front of her. Even still, I catch a glimpse of her breasts and the pale pink of her nipples. My dick hardens, and I stifle a groan.

"I thought this was a part of the kitchen," she says and I hear the drunkenness on her words. Her thick lashes flutter as I stay standing in the doorway to the wine cellar, silently.

I wait for her to peek up at me, and when she does I hold her captive with my stare. It's never made sense to me before why the expression of 'doe eyes' exists. But right here, right now, I understand. It's a glance you can't break. One that pauses time and holds you still. That's what she does to me in this moment with that gorgeous gaze.

"I swear I didn't realize," she breathes the words and licks her wine-stained lips.

"From one cell to another," I tell her and my little songbird bites down on her bottom lip to stifle a smile. "You find that funny?" I ask her as my own lips threaten to tip up.

"I would prefer this one," she tells me as a flirtatious blush creeps into her cheeks. "If you saw fit to put me in a cell again, the wine cellar would be a bit more my style."

A genuine grin pulls at my lips and I find myself walking toward her and crouching in front of her small, delicate frame. Although she seems sweet, engaging even, the nervousness is still present.

I almost ask her what's gotten her into such a pleasant mood, but the empty bottle of wine to her side and the mostly empty glass sitting next to it answer my question. Her pupils are dark and large, but the beauty and desire behind them are enticing.

"You've enjoyed yourself while I've been gone?" I ask her while cupping her cheek, but instead of leaning into me, she pulls away and moves to sit on her ass. She pulls her legs to her chest.

She shakes her head once, and the happiness leaves instantly, chilling the room and my blood.

"I have something I should tell you," she speaks to her knees with her head buried in them, "but Daniel said he wouldn't." Some of her words are slurred. And even with the cuteness of her tipsy demeanor, knowing Daniel was housing a secret with her steals any sense of humor from me. "But I should."

"Yes," I tell her as I sit on the floor in front of her, "you should." A vise grips my heart as I creep closer to her. Secrets can't be tolerated. Secrets destroy all they touch. And Daniel would keep a secret from me?

She scratches behind her ear and glances at the door before looking back at me. Her lips part, but then she simply licks them, still trying to find her words. I can hear the steady beat of her heart in rhythm with mine.

"Tell me, songbird. It will be much worse for you if you don't." A crease of sadness mars her forehead and her eyes darken with worry, but the threat was needed. And with it comes her confession.

"I cut him," she says quickly and then clears her throat. "Daniel. I held up the knife and threatened him to let me go but I didn't mean to cut him, I swear."

"You want to leave me?" I ask contemptuously. The anger has come so easily tonight, my emotions getting the best of me. And it's because of her. It's all because of Aria.

"No, I just," she swallows thickly and pushes the hair from her face. "I don't know why, but when you left me... it's different when you aren't with me." She struggles with her words and I wait a moment in silence for her to go on.

"I was angry. I wanted to leave to tell my father." She doesn't see how my body tenses and rage creeps into my expression at her confession. She will never leave me. Never. And her father can burn in hell for all I care.

Gritting my teeth, I let her continue.

"He came to talk to me, and I had a knife. I was drunk and it was stupid. Or maybe just tipsy? I'm so sorry. I didn't mean it. I'm just a mess and I don't know what's right or what I should do and I..." She trails off, her breathing and words chaotic at best.

Has Daniel really gone so soft that he would let her threaten him? The sense of disappointment in both of them is mixed, but so much stronger with Aria. She wanted to leave. I have to resist every urge to throw her back into the cell and keep her there where she doesn't have an ounce of escape.

It's only the genuine sadness in her eyes that dulls the anger and brings out the curiosity I felt when I first watched her from the monitors.

It takes a moment of heavy breathing and silence between us for me to realize that it's my fault. She wasn't ready to be left in someone else's hands. I should have known better. But things will change quickly. I nod at the thought, although my gaze stays on Aria. Soon.

"He let you cut him with a knife?" I ask her, wondering how reckless Daniel must've been.

It's because she doesn't fear him. Fear changes everything.

"Only a little," she answers in a meek voice while lifting those gorgeous eyes up to mine and I find it humorous. With a gentle smile tracing my lips, I clarify, "You cut him... but only a little?"

She dares to let the peek of a smile show, but it's quickly

gone. "I feel awful for doing it."

"You would have killed my brother?" I ask absently, making a mental note to watch the tapes of her while I was gone.

"No, but I know you'd kill mine." Her words are a well of sadness, but also of acceptance.

"You have no brother," I tell her as if her statement is irrelevant, but she's right. There are no limits to what I've done and what I'm about to do. There is mercy for her, but not for anyone else.

"You really tried to leave me?" A spike punctures through my chest as I voice it out loud. Earlier, I was more concerned that she shared a secret with Daniel. But the fact remains that she tried to run away. That she wanted to leave me and was willing to kill to do it.

"It was an awful attempt," she tells me as if it makes it better. And a part of me softens at her response. "I'm sorry. I'm sorry about it all. I think I'm going crazy," her words come out breathily as she drops her head back to lean against the wall. "You've made me crazy, Carter. All I am is sorry. It's all I know how to be anymore."

With my hand cupping her jaw, I wait for her to look at me with glassy eyes on the verge of tears. "No, my songbird. All you are... is mine."

"Yes," she says simply. The acknowledgement giving me a headier rush than I've ever felt.

My head nods on its own. "I didn't think you'd dare to be

so bold while I was gone."

"I'm sorry." Fear traces her whisper.

"I didn't want to punish you tonight of all nights," I tell her, letting my fingers run along the necklace she wears, "I had different plans in mind." My dick is already hard as I consider what to do with her. "But you tried to leave me and there's no greater sin than that."

"Please," she whimpers as I shush her. "I don't want to go back." She doesn't cower from my touch; she welcomes it as I rest a hand on her bare shoulder, my fingers skimming under the fabric of her shirt. Her mesmerizing hazel eyes stare into mine and beg me for mercy.

"Didn't I tell you your next offense would lead to the cell?" I remind her with a question and her face crumples. She inches toward me, both of her hands on my thighs as she begs me, "Please." Her fingers slip across the expensive fabric of my pants as she crawls between my legs, begging me for forgiveness. How I've dreamed of her like this. Just like this.

"What would you do to stay with me?" I ask her, wanting to give her the mercy she begs for. I've never felt it so strongly before.

Her chest rises and falls heavily. "Anything," she answers me quickly with desperation.

"Not to stay out of the cell, but to stay in my bed. There is a difference, Aria."

Her expression falls and she struggles to voice what she's

thinking. Dread seeps into my gut as she fails to answer me, but with that soft voice of hers, it leaves me at once.

Her fingers lace through the necklace as she says, "It's only when you're gone that I remember."

"What do you mean?"

Her voice wavers as she tries to explain. "I don't want you to leave me. It's harder for me when you do."

"I asked you what you would do--"

"And I said anything," she cuts me off and I can feel my brow pinch together as I look over every inch of her expression to gauge her sincerity. "When you're with me, I know that I can't leave, and I don't want to even try. But when you're gone... it's harder. So, I don't want to leave you. I don't want you to leave me."

She's a siren. I see it so clearly. It's her beauty, her broken strength, her denial, and her acceptance. It all calls to me and I will do anything I can to wrap my grip tighter around my songbird while she sings beautiful lullabies.

"Tomorrow night, you'll come to dinner with me. Kneeling beside me. You will obey. You will sit beside me, proud to be mine." She nods her head as if she's accepting a punishment, but this is so much more than that. "You'll do as I say. Every fucking thing I tell you to do." I emphasize each word, my finger running up and down her throat. "In front of my family and guests, you will show them how willing you are to obey me."

"Yes, Carter."

The way her breathing catches and she swallows the eagerness of accepting the punishment, almost makes me feel guilty for what I say next. Almost. "And tonight, you will sleep in the cell for daring to take advantage of the freedom I've given you."

"Yes, Carter," she replies although her words crack and her eyes close in agony. Her thick lashes flutter, as she opens her eyes again and she stares deeply into my own, waiting for more. The deep well of loneliness is already settling into her gaze. The look of sadness is something I've seen before, but in her eyes, it looks so beautiful.

"You'll stay there until I feel you've learned your lesson."

She nods and wipes the tear from under her right eye, but dutifully answers, "Yes, Carter."

My own breathing quickens at the thought of having her to myself before sending her away. "As for right now, you'll lie across my lap, feeling my hard cock dig into your belly as I punish you, spanking your bare ass and playing with your cunt until I feel you've paid enough for the offense of trying to leave me."

"I will," she says softly and raises her head to meet my gaze. When her eyes meet mine, she nods in agreement. "I will," she repeats breathlessly.

The command falls instantly from me. "Tell me that your cunt is mine to play with."

"My cunt is yours to play with." And her obedience falls from her lips just the same.

"And your ass?" I prompt.

"It's yours." There's no hesitation in her voice.

"And what about these lips of yours?" I question her in a deep voice ragged with desire as my thumb traces her pouty lips.

"Whatever you'd like to do with them," she whispers against my touch.

"Lift up your dress and lie here," I tell her as I sit on the ground of the wine cellar, too eager to have my hands on her to move us to the cell.

Her movements are rushed and reckless as she pulls the cotton dress up and moves to my lap. Her hips are balanced on my right thigh, but I move her ass to the center, forcing her to yelp as she tries to brace herself with her hands.

"Behind your back," I command her, and it takes a moment. Her hair is everywhere, but I slip it over one shoulder, taking my time to gather it together before grabbing both of her wrists in one of my hands. My fingers easily slip down her panties, the lace fabric almost tearing, but I'm careful with it, letting my touch send goosebumps flowing over every inch of her skin.

She moans slightly, already enjoying her punishment. But I'll enjoy it more.

With my hand rubbing a circle on her ass cheek, I tell her,

"I think you misbehave just so I can punish you."

She shakes her head, writhing over my lap and making her hair toss slightly. "I don't want to upset you." Her words are soft and saddened, but her whimpers speak of nothing but pleasure.

The first smack is light and followed by my grabbing her ass and then smacking the other cheek harder. Her body bucks, but I don't even get a gasp.

Leaning to my left, I see her eyes shut tightly and her teeth digging into her bottom lip. I let my fingers slip to her cunt, and my cock aches with the pain to be inside of her.

"So tight," I tell her with reverence in my tone and then rock her, so she can feel my cock.

She only moans and waits for more, but her teeth let up slightly while I take my time with her.

"How many do you think, my Aria?" I ask her and just as her lips part, my hand pulls back and I whip her ass with an open hand that leaves my skin stinging with pain. She cries out, throwing her head back as the pain and pleasure mix and my fingers dip back to her cunt.

"I asked how many?" My voice is calm but deadly. Inside I'm burning hot with a desperate need.

"How many--" she starts to answer me, and I spank her other cheek even harder than the last, forcing tears to her eyes. The sharp, sweet pain travels from my palm up my arm. Gripping her reddened skin, I wait for her to answer but with her eyes watering and her breath taken from her, all she does is part her lips to breathe.

"Answer me, Aria." Before my words are finished she says as quickly as she can, "However many you'd like."

A beat passes where she hangs her head to suck in a breath. Another beat passes where I pull my hand away from her skin and watch as she tenses on my lap.

The rapid succession of my hand hitting her tender skin over and over again until my arm is screaming with pain and my hand feels nearly numb passes in a whirlwind.

Her cries get louder as she fights me in my lap, naturally wanting to pull away from me. I nearly lose my grip on her wrists, but I manage to keep her steady and where I need her to be, so I can fulfill her punishment.

Her ass is bright red and my skin humming with a delightful sting by the time I slip my fingers back to her soaking wet cunt. Her body shudders and her yelp of pain turns to a sinful moan.

Over and over I spank her viciously, the underside of her ass, the right cheek, the left one... and then her pussy. My hand's wet with her arousal as she trembles beneath me.

My fingers dip into her pussy with each smack, giving her only the tiniest bit of penetration. The intensity of the teasing bends her back even farther and her lust-filled gaze stares back at me with her strangled moans of pleasure and pain echoing off the walls of the cellar.

"Good girl." I praise her and watch as she peers up at me with a wondering look in her eyes and her cheeks tearstained.

"Tonight, I'm going to fuck you into that mattress on the floor like I should have the moment I got my hands on you."

Her pussy clenches around my fingertips and I reward her by pushing them in deeper and stroking her front wall.

Her back arches and I have to push her shoulder down to keep her right where I want her as I pull my touch away from her in order to leave her wanting. Her small moan of frustration is met with another slap of my hand on her bright red skin. Smack!

Her head flies back and those gorgeous lips of hers part with a deep gasp of longing. It's no longer pain. She's too close to the edge of pleasure to feel anything but.

Soothing the pain of the smack with my hand, I rub her right cheek and then pull back for one more strike.

"You would have learned sooner if I'd been rougher with you, wouldn't you?"

She moans her answer with her eyes closed and her body still, knowing another punishing blow is coming, "Yes, Carter."

Her answer is absent of sincerity. She'd tell me whatever I wanted to hear right now as she sits on the edge of pleasure and pain.

The days come back to me. Each of them and what I'd planned to do with her is in such stark contrast to what I've done. I let the fingers of my right hand trail over her ass, my blunt nails gently scraping along her tender skin and making her squirm on my lap. My left hand grips her throat, finally releasing her wrists, and I pull back, forcing her to look at me.

Her hazel eyes are filled with longing and lust. The haze is a fog in the forest. Unable to see, but so tempted to go forward.

"I should have fucked you so much sooner."

I remember that first day, how she screamed and cried for me to let her go, back when I hated her and she hated me.

Even with my tight grip on her throat, with my touch sending sparks through her body, she forces her head to shake, not taking her eyes from mine.

"No," she whispers, and my dick hardens, even more, begging me to punish her for daring to defy me. But then she adds, "This is how it was supposed to be."

Her breathing is heavy as she closes her eyes, her body bowed on my lap. She's completely at my mercy and her pouty lips are there for the taking.

All of her. Every piece of her is mine and she knows it.

Mine.

CHAPTER 28

ARIA

Yesterday was full of regret.

The moment I saw Carter again, I wish I'd taken back those hours he was gone.

He always keeps his word. And true to form, he took me back to the cell and fucked me on the mattress. Maybe it was the drunkenness, maybe it was something else, but the fear of the cell was absent and instead, I did everything I could to please him. My body begged me to.

Not because I felt the need to obey.

I wanted him to kiss me.

I needed him to. And every time his lips trailed down my neck, I tried to capture them. Tried and failed. He knows I want him though. A shudder runs through my body at the thought and it's met with the dull ache between my thighs.

He fucked me until I couldn't move anymore and even as I laid on my belly on the mattress, unable to grip onto it, unable to keep my back arched as he commanded me to. Even then he rutted behind me, pistoning into me and giving me a punishing fuck.

Last night I was his whore. He balled my hair into his fist and pulled back so he could rake his teeth along my neck and force my body however he wanted it.

And I wanted nothing more.

The realization should startle me more, but instead, all I can think about is that he knows I want him to kiss me, and yet he didn't let me.

It's different when he's with me. The security I have with him is everything.

The sane part of me knows it's not healthy and that I should keep fighting, but the sane part of me is the only part of me that's held captive in this reality. If only I let it go, I feel free.

Free enough to feel safe for another day.

Free enough to know that what happens in the war will happen regardless of whether I'm here or not.

Free enough to slip on the dress that Carter's laid out for me and stare at the image of a beautiful woman in the mirror. One who I envy. One I can't believe is me.

With my hair smoothed and clipped at the side, the bit of makeup adding a definition of beauty to my porcelain skin, I feel so much like a songbird who sings soft melodies of hope, with her wings clipped in a gilded cage.

My fingers graze over the delicate lace and my eyes close, remembering last night.

The bruise on my ass sends a reminder of the pain through me as I smooth the soft lace down my curves. The sensation is directly linked to my clit and instantly my body begs for more. For me to put an ounce of pressure against the bruise.

A soft breath leaves me, a wanting one at that, and when I open my eyes, Carter is standing in front of me.

My heart slams and then does a soft trot. As if it's galloping toward him, even though he's the one walking toward me.

Each step is deliberate, but with a softness I've never seen from him and it captures every bit of my thoughts.

"You look beautiful, songbird," he says, and his voice is like velvet as he rounds me. His steps echo in the bedroom as he walks in a half circle and stops at my back.

I can hear his breathing hitch as he pulls at the lace, sliding it up my backside and sending a thrilling shiver up my body. His fingertips trail ever so gently along the marks. "Beautiful," he remarks before hiding them under the lace once again.

"Thank you," I dare to whisper, meeting his gaze as he walks to stand in front of me. My fingers slip to the hem of the dress, toying with it to hide the anxiousness of wanting to touch him as he's just touched me. I'm not allowed to today.

When he opened the door to the cell, he told me if I obeyed every wish of his today, I would never see the cell again.

One day, and the rules of the game change forever.

A million thoughts are scattered through my mind, but only one of them matters.

"I'll be good tonight," I tell him in a voice I don't recognize. One of obedience, but also strength. "I won't disappoint you." A past version of me would slit my throat before letting herself hear those words. There's only a faint blip of pain in my heart at the realization.

The earlier version of me was foolish.

This version of me will survive. And this version has the audacity to admit that I enjoy it. Every fucking bit of it. To be wanted by a man so powerful who wants for nothing is a heady feeling.

"Aria," Carter says my name in a way that makes fear blossom deep in my gut. "You're going to want to defy me," he tells me, and the worry shows on my face. I can feel it tugging my lips down as it dries out my throat. He stalks in a circle around me, occasionally picking at the lace of the dress. They're cages. Each of the pieces of lace is a birdcage. And there's never been a dress that's adorned my body as beautifully as this one does.

"You may even hate me," he says in a purely seductive cadence. His hot breath tickles the bare skin of my neck as he whispers at the shell of my ear, "But you will obey me."

I nod my head and then croak out, "Yes, Carter." It's so silent in the room with neither of us speaking, moving or even daring to breathe. It's so silent I swear the darkness itself could whisper and I would hear its threatening tongue.

"Your necklace suits this dress perfectly," Carter says out loud although I don't think the words were meant for me.

Absently, I roll one of the pearls between my fingers and then feel the thin chain slide under my thumb as it moves to the diamond teardrop. It feels heavier tonight. Everything feels heavier when Carter looks at me like he is now.

With dark eyes that pin me in place and keep me still, right where he wants me. It's a silly thing, how the same gaze that once caused fear to ripple through my body now only heats my core and begs me to bend at the knees for him.

"Thank--"

Carter places a finger against my lips, silencing me. The small touch is addictive and the tension of the dinner tonight amplifies.

"Remember what I told you last night." He speaks as he toys with the necklace, holding the large diamond and lifting the weight from me. "You will kneel beside me, and you will obey every command."

Instantly my body heats. I worry my bottom lip between my teeth, wanting to ask him so many questions, but I already know he won't answer. There's only one thing to say. "Yes, Carter."

A moment passes, his eyes searching my gaze for something and I can hardly breathe.

"After tonight, no one will question that you're mine." His eyes darken and the flecks of gold that are buried beneath the coal there turn to fire. A fire that ignites my own and soothes the worries.

"Come with me," he commands me as he reaches for my hand.

CHAPTER 29

CARTER

My walk is calm and steady, even as Aria freezes.

The cocky smirk stays plastered on my lips, even as sickness stirs in my gut.

Every bit of my body is screaming to act, but this is for her. It's all for her.

"Come," I command Aria as she stares straight ahead at the entrance to the dining hall. Her chest rises in slow motion as her lips part with the hint of a shaky breath. "Aria," I say, and her name slips from me like an admonishment, "I said come." The demand is there, but the look she gives me in return is one of defiance and betrayal. There's so much hate in the dark greens and ambers of her eyes that I almost regret this.

But she needs this. That hate for me won't be there for long.

Stephan and Romano's shared rumble of deep laughter is the only sound in the large room as they see her. With the blood-red velvet curtains shut tightly, the only light in the room shines down from the scattered crystals on the chandelier.

The smell of beef wellington, seated beautifully at the center of the table, greets us as we enter the room. The light shines off the butcher's knife beside it.

Aria's walk is hesitant but she obeys me, even if there are tears in her eyes.

"I was beginning to think I'd have to come up and get you," Jase says as I take Aria's hand in mine and motion for her to kneel beside my chair across from Stephan. Her palm is clammy, and her grip tight as she lowers herself to the floor. The pain I feel for her is nothing compared to what she'll have in only moments.

As quickly as she can, she tears her hand from mine. And again, laughter from the two guests echoes off the walls.

"Still so defiant." Romano's eyes sparkle, but I ignore him, taking my seat.

I hate that for the moment I can't keep my hand on hers, but soon I'll have her again.

"No need," I tell Jase, meeting his gaze and forcing a smile on my lips that grows as I turn my attention to Stephan, nodding a greeting and then turn to Romano. "Thank you for coming, gentlemen."

"The pleasure is all mine," Stephan says at the same time as Romano nods his head, the thin smile growing on his lips and turning wicked.

"It's a delight to see you've taken a liking to our gift."

Anger burns deep in my chest at the memory of him having his hands on her only weeks ago, but it stays where it is as I return his smile, placing my hand on the back of Aria's head. She remains stiff, not leaning into my touch, which only intensifies the fire inside of me. But I will have patience, even if she tests me.

"I wish I could see her better," Stephan says, sitting up from his seat for a moment and making a comical face. Jase gives him a bit of laughter, I'm sure because he knows what's coming. He'll enjoy this, but not nearly as much as I will.

"No sense of humor?" Stephan speaks to Daniel and then glances at Declan, both of them quiet. It's only the seven of us in the room, although the kitchen is abuzz with the sound of dishes being plated. And the men waiting for my order.

"I know a few jokes," Daniel says wryly, but then he picks up his drink and leaves the unspoken words hanging in the air. Romano's shoulders stiffen and a hard gaze meets his eyes.

"Come up here, Aria," I say and pat my lap and then glance at Stephan. "I'd like for our guests to see you better."

From the corner of my eye, I see Romano's tension ease. The room is silent, so silent I can hear my songbird swallow as she stands up on weak legs. I'm quick to pull her into my lap, pressing my hand against her ass and reminding her of last night. Her eyes widen, and she gasps, thrilling the men she doesn't dare look at.

"Excuse her," I speak to no one in particular. "She's not used to company."

With all eyes on her, I place her exactly how I'd like her, nestling her ass into my crotch and wrapping my arm around her waist. "Relax," I whisper into her ear, knowing full well the other men can hear me. Her hair tickles against my jaw and shoulder as I move it from one side of her back to the other so I can expose her neck.

"You can't say hello to an old friend?" Stephan asks.

"If I recall, she's more fond of begging." Romano's comment doesn't go unnoticed.

"She's a little frightened," I say before kissing the crook of her neck and feeling her body relax for the first time, although I know the moment will be gone before I'd like.

"One of the many Talverys who will fall to their knees," Stephan gloats and raises his glass to toast, but I don't reciprocate.

"I thought she would, but she betrayed me last night," I tell them and reach for a goblet of water.

"Betrayed?" Romano's voice is low.

I nod and look to see how my brothers react to my words.

"I thought she was doing well?" Jase comments and leans forward in his seat to look at Aria, his stare commanding her to look at him, which she does, but only for a moment. Her head is held high, but her glassy gaze stares at nothing.

"She tried to kill Daniel," I tell Jase and he gives me a look of shock but then turns to Daniel, who's smiling.

"Kill you?" he questions Daniel.

"As if she could," he says, leaning back in his seat. Aria struggles to breathe as we talk about her in front of her like her presence is a meaningless joke. But everything has a purpose.

"It was only a knife." Daniel looks at me as he answers, and I reach for the one in front of me.

"This one?" I ask him, and Aria rocks forward a moment, her ability to stay strong being questioned. When I peer up at her, her eyes are shut tightly. "Look at me, Aria." My words are lethal on my tongue.

Instantly, her eyes open and a scattering of tears lines her lashes. Instead of wiping them away, I hold up the knife and ask, "This one?"

She shakes her head gently. "No," she says, the word a mere whisper. I can feel the pounding of her heart.

"Take it," I demand as I grab her hand and put it over the handle of the knife. "Would you like to use it on him now?" I ask her.

"No," she says and her voice trembles, but again she shakes her head and answers me. "How about on me?" I offer her. "Would you like to slit my throat, Aria?"

"No." Her answer is a barely spoken breath and her grip

on the knife loosens.

"I told Daniel this morning," I begin, addressing Romano to my right and giving him my full attention, "that it was his fault. There was no fear of him and what he'd do to her."

Romano considers me, his brow raising and his lips turning down into a frown before he nods in agreement. "Fear is powerful."

"I choose other tactics," Daniel speaks up and then looks at Aria as he adds, "I let her do what she thought she needed to, so she could at least feel that she'd tried." His voice is neutral, devoid of the empathy I know he has for her. It's all a show. That's the real difference between us; Daniel likes to hide behind an image.

I am the image of what's to be feared. It exists in my being and there's no hiding it.

"Do you remember me, Aria?" Stephan dares to ask her, leaning across the table to be every bit closer to her that he can.

"Oh, she does," I answer for her as she struggles to respond. "My poor Aria, I know this is hard for you," I say and hold her tighter, although she's stiff doing her best to stay seated on my lap.

"I imagine it is," Stephan says and then adds, "She's grown to be just as beautiful as her mother."

My blood sings with both rage and vengeance, and it's a feeling I adore. A smile creeps across my lips as I confide in him, "She sings for me, but the memory of you is strong enough to stop it." I turn to Aria, letting my finger trail over her shoulder to slip a lock of hair to her back and then turn to Stephan. "I can't have that."

Confusion mars his face for a moment and I let time pass for a moment in deadly silence.

"I could give her a different memory to hold onto," Stephan suggests and the laugh that creeps from Romano's gut is tight with tension.

"I don't believe Carter enjoys sharing," Romano comments, but I hold up my hand to stop him, speaking only to Stephan.

"I do believe she needs a different memory. I'm tired of hearing her cry out in her sleep." As I speak, Aria's expression crumples and I pull her closer to me, forcing her back to my chest and whisper in her ear, "Should I let Stephan fuck you?" I don't let them see the anger, the hate, the deep-seated pain of watching my songbird relive the memories in front of her tormentor. They can't see yet, but they will suffer. I swear they will pay.

Deep in my core, I have the fear of breaking Aria, of pushing her too hard, but she needs this.

"Carter," Jase warns, and I only shoot him a gaze of contempt. If this is to go as planned, Romano is the witness whose testimony matters. His perception is the only one that matters.

Aria breaks down at the mere question, her reality again

failing her. Each bit of her shatters with hope fading from her very existence. It's then I know I've truly broken her and the beautiful shards of what used to be Aria Talvery can fill the crevice of my soul she broke long ago. And I can use those pieces how I'd like. Creating perfection in her from what's been broken.

As she gasps an answer, a plea from her lips that only I can hear, I pull her tighter to me, feeling her warmth and her small body pressed securely against mine. The knife is still in her hand, although weakly held.

"You still have the knife, Aria," I remind her. "Would you like to cut me now?" As I ask her the question, her hazel-green eyes strike me with every ounce of pain she feels at this moment. "Why are you doing this to me?" she asks, her small voice revealing her agony.

I let my fingers slip up her dress as Romano says something I don't care to listen to.

Letting my lips trail along the back of her neck, I whisper just for her. "Do you think I'd let him fuck you?" I ask her and press my fingers to her clit, forcing her to push back and feel my cock on her bruised ass, hard at the very thought of what's coming. "That I would let him even imagine taking what's mine?" The hiss of my voice travels throughout the dining room, but I'm certain no one could know for sure what I've asked her.

Her eyes, still shining with unshed tears, finally meet

mine and stare back at me as she whispers, "No."

A smile threatens to pull at my lips and I let it as Romano and Stephan cluck their tongues in disapproval, as if they have any control at all over her. As if they know what's coming.

I rock her into my lap again and the sweet gasp that parts her lips brings a light to her eyes. A light that I've given her. Only me.

Bringing my lips to the shell of her ear, I whisper, "Do you think I'd *ever*," I stress the word, "let him touch you?" As I prompt her, the demeanor of my guests change.

"No," she says with the strength of realization. My sweet girl. I watch as her breathing calms and she glances at Stephan and then Romano before looking back at me and answering me again, her head shaking and letting those locks play around her bare shoulders. "No," she repeats softly.

"She's rather bold, don't you think?" Romano asks Jase, who doesn't respond to him.

"I love how strong she is," I say aloud, ignoring the comments from Stephan at the end of the table for a moment before adding, "Her will was difficult to break, but it was worth it."

Declan speaks up, tired of the show I imagine. He has no patience and he states pointedly, "The dinner is getting cold."

"Of course." I lean back in my seat and splay my hand against Aria's stomach to push her small body against mine. "Would you like to carve the meat, Aria?" I ask her and glance behind me toward the kitchen. "Bring out the plates in just a moment," I call out and catch Romano's gaze. "This chef is to die for."

"I can hardly wait," he says beneath his breath.

"Aria," I tell them, "will cut the wellington and serve us, I think." A half grin ticks up the corners of my lips as Romano smiles.

"I didn't expect this from you," he tells me, and I cock a brow at him. "I didn't think you enjoyed this as much as you seem to."

My grin widens. "You have no idea how much I enjoy this." Tonight, my songbird will be changed forever. And I'm the one who will give it to her. She will never fear anyone but me ever again.

"You have her sit at the table?" Stephan questions me with a glint of humor in his eyes. His thin lips twitch into a smile and I manage a smile back, remembering that this is for her. She's the one to do it. My grip on her waist tightens, to keep me from ruining everything.

"You do as you'd like in your home, but do not question me in mine." My words are sharp and not to be taken lightly. They force the smile off his pale face while Romano coughs at the head of the table.

"I think he only means that we were expecting to see her on the floor... where slaves belong."

Picking up the large butcher knife on the table, I put

the knife firmly in Aria's hand and command her to carve the beef wellington. She can barely reach, and I do my best to balance her as she reaches over the table, the sharp blade piercing the puff pastry shell with a slight crack that's audible in the silent room.

My breathing comes in harder and harder, knowing what's next. I can taste the sweetness of it already as the meat falls onto the platter.

"Carter has a soft spot for her, I think," Jase offers, and he and Daniel share a look. One of my brothers on each side of me. Both of them ready for when I cue the kitchen.

"I want a nice meal, for fuck's sake," I say with a touch of humor to break the tension and put both Stephan and Romano at ease. "We start a war tomorrow. And technically, shots have already been fired," I say, and shrug then place a small bit of meat onto the platter as Aria's movements become strained.

"Yes. Here's to victory," Romano says, raising the glass of champagne in front of him. The bubbly liquid rises in the air, and with it, both of his hands. It's like I'm watching in slow motion as I turn my attention to Stephan and see him do the same. An empty hand palm up on the table and his other raised in the air, holding a glass.

"Cheers, bring out the dinner," I call out as I raise my glass, not bothering to reach for my gun.

My voice rings out and our men from the kitchen bring out the serving dishes. My closest men, disguised as servers, quickly make their way around the room with their trays.

They unveil each of the covered platters at once to reveal their guns, aimed at both Romano and Stephan. All while Aria's carving the meat with shaky hands.

Stephan and Romano both suck in a breath but keep their hands raised even as curses fill the air, as do the sound of pistols being cocked.

Aria drops the knife on the table, her shoulders hunched and a squeal of both terror and surprise forcing her backward and into my arms. I wish I could have warned her, but Romano is going to live to tell the tale.

Her shoulders are cold in my embrace as I pull her close and whisper, "You're all right."

All three of my brothers raise their loaded guns, but I keep my hands on Aria, still trembling. Declan, seated at the opposite head, keeps his gun pointed at Romano and my other two brothers keep theirs pointed at Stephan as they face him.

"What the fuck is this?" Romano is quick to speak with indignation and attempts to lower his arm. My eyes pierce into Stephan's, who's staring straight at me with a bitter hate that I'm used to seeing from men I've fucked over. It's always followed by the milky gaze of dead eyes. He doesn't dare lower his arm. Because he knows the truth better than Romano does.

I hear the distinctive sound of a gun with a silencer going off, but I don't bother to look and verify that the bullet landed just behind Romano as a warning shot. My eyes stay fixed on Stephan's. Just as his are on me.

"This is a show for you, Romano," I finally speak when he stands abruptly. "Help him sit, Jase."

Without a word, my brother rises and I can just barely see Aria in my periphery. My sweet, haunted girl. She grips the table and watches intently as Jase pulls out the chair for Romano, waiting for him to sit a few feet away from the table where his hands can easily be seen.

Jase stays behind him, his gun still trained on Romano although now he could easily shoot Stephan as well. But his death is for Aria, and Aria alone.

"The knife, Aria." I address only her. She's so small on my lap as she looks at me and then slowly around the room. She's hesitant to pick the knife back up and the cursing yell from Stephan nearly startles her into dropping it again.

The rage in my blood turns from a simmer to a boil. "Even now he holds a fear over you, my Aria," I tell her in a low voice of reprimand. "I won't allow it."

I can feel her skin turn cold as she waits for my command. She's barely breathing, still scared and confused. With the knife in her hand, I pull her back into my lap, taking my time to calm her so she can see clearly.

Fear can cloud everything, turning reality into falsehoods.

"Are you mad at me, songbird?" I ask her gently, cupping her jaw in my hand. I can feel her swallow tightly and peek back at Stephan before looking at me. "Why?" she asks me with such sadness.

"You needed this," I whisper against her lips, nearly pressing mine to hers in an effort for her to understand how crucial this moment is, both for her and for us.

Her bottom lip quivers as tears prick the back of her eyes. "I thought you were giving me to him," she confesses as her voice cracks and her shoulders shudder.

Gripping her tighter I speak clearly, loud enough for everyone in this room to hear. "You are mine and Romano lied to me when he gave me to you," I hiss.

"Bullshit!" Romano dares to interrupt me and my hackles rise, the anger brimming. But I'll deal with him once I'm through with Aria. She will always come first.

"You were damaged." Her expression crumples at my words, shame filling her hazel eyes as I add, "You were so fucking broken I couldn't have my hand in it." I turn my head to sneer at Stephan. "Not when someone else has such control over you."

"I'm sorry," she whispers, and the tip of the knife hits the table as her grip loosens.

"Did I tell you to drop the knife?" I ask her and instead of taking the hint and holding it tighter, she drops it to the table, covering her face with her hands and leaning into my chest.

"I really thought..." she pauses as her chest heaves and I give her this moment. I comfort her and make the men wait.

They will wait for her. And so will I.

For this I've waited so long already, another minute can be spared for her pain.

"I thought," she continues to stammer, and I kiss her hair, rubbing her back as she tells me, "I thought you were done with me."

Pulling at her shoulders, I force her to arm's length in my lap. "Never," I tell her with all sincerity, feeling the truth down to my core, coursing through my blood and in every thought I could ever have.

Aria's breathing calms as she stares into my eyes, while a softness I've never felt drifts over me. "You scared me," she whispers.

Running the tip of my nose against hers, I whisper against her lips, "It's a gift for you."

When I pull away, her eyes are still closed, but slowly they open and I nod toward the knife.

"Kill him, Aria."

Romano curses, but one of my men presses the barrel of his gun to his head.

"Pick up the knife and end him."

I watch Aria's shaky fingers pick up the knife, and then she stares at her prey. He scowls at her, but she doesn't back down. Her chest heaves again and the way she holds her chin up lets me know she's scared but doing her damnedest not to be.

Fear can never hide though.

"I won't be with you if you don't," I tell her and instantly regret the words. Her eyes widen, and she sucks in a breath. "I can't let you continue like this," I tell her, wishing I could take back the first words I gave her.

Her eyes flicker from me to Stephan and she nods her head slightly, but still, she doesn't move.

Even knowing she has the knife in her hand, I lean forward and rest my head against her chest. "This is for you, Aria," I whisper in the hot space between us. "It's all for you."

Inhaling her scent and feeling her body against mine, I kiss her throat and move to the crook of her slender neck. Her nails dig into my shoulder as she gasps.

It's an apology for the threat I just made that never should have left me.

My lips slip down her shoulder and she moans softly, relaxing into me as my hands travel up her waist.

"Kill him, Aria," I command her and continue kissing her neck, my touch turning ravenous.

Raking my teeth down her jaw, I worship her.

My brothers are witnesses to what I'd do to have her be completely mine. Romano and the dead fuck Stephan watch with a series of slurs and profanity.

Let them all see. Let the entire fucking world see.

My cock is hard when I pull away, seeing her breathless and in need.

"First, you take care of him." I nod toward Stephan and

then tell her, "And then you will be truly mine."

Aria's nod is swift and she's quick this time to leave my lap, although her touch lingers on my shoulder as she steadies herself.

Three guns are pointed at Stephan, but he's only looking at her as she rounds the table. I follow her at a distance, giving her this.

Stephan's smile is grim and unnerving as he sneers, "She'll never do it. Just shoot--"

Before he can get the last word out, Aria whips her hand through the air, slicing his neck open and forcing blood to pour from his neck. As his hands reach up to his throat, she screams a bloodcurdling sound, slicing again in the same pattern. Only this time, it cuts through his hands, nearly severing one of his fingers.

She doesn't stop. She stabs frantically into his chest, hitting his arm, his shoulder, his throat again. Her aim is reckless, and my men take a step back, blood drenching his shirt and spraying from his cuts.

She's savage in the stabs. Chaotic even. For a moment, I want to tear the knife from her for fear of her cutting herself.

She screams out as the knife pierces through the expensive fabric and into his soft flesh, the blood seeping through his clothes. The cry from her is sickening. Not because of the piercing scream, but because of the overt sadness. She kills him with her pain.

"Let it out," I say without conscious consent. I can see Daniel turn his attention from her to me, but I ignore him. None of them matter right now.

She needs this more than anything.

Romano stands from his seat, backing away and it's only then that I break my focus on Aria.

"Sit," I practically snarl. The anger is mostly because he dared distract me from this.

He grits his teeth and feigns irritation as he slowly obeys me, but he can't deny the utter fear I can see in his gaze.

With both hands on the armrests, he slowly takes his seat and I can focus on Aria again.

Her energy has waned and she's silent as tears stream down her face. Her small body looks weaker and weaker, but she doesn't stop stabbing into Stephan's lifeless body. She's obviously exhausted, but she doesn't stop.

Not until I give her the command, my low voice foreboding and dominating in the silent room. "Aria. Give me the knife."

Her wild eyes glance at me, only for a moment as the knife trembles in her hand and she shakes her head, no.

"Aria," I raise my voice, forcing it to echo in the room. The only sounds I can hear are the blood rushing in my ears and Aria's ragged breathing as I grit my teeth and tell her one last time. "Give. Me. The knife."

TO BE CONTINUED

Carter and Aria's story continues in

HEARTLESS!!

ABOUT THE AUTHOR

Thank you so much for reading my romances. I'm just a stay at home Mom and an avid reader turned Author and I couldn't be happier.

I hope you love my books as much as I do!

More by Willow Winters
www.willowwinterswrites.com/books